Dream, Again

Reinterpreting the American Dream:

Through Founder's Eyes

By Joey LeTourneau

"Hope Breathes Through Those Who Choose
To Be Awakened..."

Joey LeTourneau

Copyright © 2013 Joey LeTourneau

Imagi-Nations LLC

Inquiries contact: joey.letourneau@gmail.com

ISBN-10: 061593420X
ISBN-13: 978-0615934204

Dedication:

To my kids…

I want to be more like each of you. You inspire me to live every dream and purpose I have been created for. And I can only hope, and pray, that I will always do the same for you. I love you!

Acknowledgments:

A huge thank you to all those who have helped birth this book: Destiny, as always you've held up my arms in more ways than I can say throughout this project; I love you. Mom and Jackie, your willingness to be a sounding board enriches everything. Eleanor Perry-Smith, thank you very much for sharing your expertise, you made such a difference. Caleb, La Vonne, Amber, and Cindy, I can't thank you enough for being early readers and encouragers in the journey, you have been invaluable to its process, and to me personally. Jason, Stan, Jim, Ty & Kira, you have each strengthened me incredibly in different ways as this book has come together. And I must acknowledge, even if not by name, the many who have helped me to dream, those of you who have supported us and stood behind my family and I while we've carved out that river life, those who've helped stripes become scars, and believed in us and journeyed with us as we learn to scale the skies. Thank you.

CONTENTS

"Hope is the thing with feathers

That perches in the soul

And sings the tune without words

And never stops at all."

- Emily Dickinson

Introduction:
Skies, Scars & Stripes

"Freedom is never more than one generation away from extinction. We didn't pass it to our children in the bloodstream. It must be fought for, protected, and handed on for them to do the same." - Ronald Reagan

I was born with the skies in my blood. And born into a nation taught to reach for such. Unfortunately, that has led to many reaching for the dream within me, without ever touching those skies for themselves. My family line was a symbol created by the pioneers who helped birth this great nation. But I have to say it hasn't always *felt* like a great journey, even when it truly was.

The skies, though smooth to the seer who dreams of them, have been like treacherously stormy waters as I've sought to live them out on land among men. The picture or impression of those skies cannot be understood without feeling them under your very own wings. I look up at the clear blue and become jealous, jealous for the life that is still very much alive within me, though kept by man's limited definition of freedom. My journey is one of great favor, illustrious clouds, horizons that can be but a floor and a story not relegated to being part of a skyscraper, but one that is best defined by these scars and stripes that have been emblazoned on my very own wings.

I've watched man build up towards those skies that are alive in me. But nothing can replace the journey that those same skies would actually allow if only asked. I wouldn't let go of one of these scars, nor the blood stained stripes they once left if it meant I had to let go of the path required to get here. Such great price always has a greater reward at the end. Many often quote the renowned saying that the whole is greater than the sum of its parts. Well, I wouldn't have the whole without the sum of my journey in between, and they aren't parts, they are part of me. That is where my true skies fling wide, and where I will never cease to fly. Nothing can remove those skies from inside me. I will always be free to fly; while knowing that it's these scars that give me strength to lift my wings.

My name is Founder. You may have met me from a distance in any number of places, the dollar bill, or any variety of seals and crests still littered across our great nation. My family line enthroned me as the symbol of a freedom whose truth has become scarce these days, a means vs. an end, a lone, high perch plucked for the price of trading in our wings. I've got the scars to prove it. And my wings, that which could have actually lifted me higher than that forsaken perch, were nearly lost in the process.

I became comfortable you see, and abandoned my pioneering edge. I once danced upon the skies with the greatest of freedom, led by unparalleled vision, yet even the quality of such esteemed traits weren't enough to keep me from blending in captive to the culture of the wolves. Their lure was subtle, and their prowess for deception had kept me blind. I was lost inside myself long before those stripes of blood threatened to permanently dismember my freedom. But, if not for those scars and stripes, I wouldn't be qualified to lead you today. Each scar is a chapter in my story, but even more so the final healing of my old wounds turned scars can be felt through those I have since met, and led. And the bloodstained stripes are now but wells of ink I use to write to those like you, like my friend, Will, who joins me in sharing both our journey's with you now.

Chapter 1:
Before Hope

"Whenever you find yourself on the side of the majority, it is time to pause and reflect." - Mark Twain

The vote still wasn't finalized, but the race was clearly over, and so went the hope in the Dowd household. Hope hadn't been lost with the wanting political party, rather, it crashed with the division in our home. My family, specifically Mom and Dad, were split in their politics, thus, they were split in their hope. Different circumstances demanded different answers. And politics was their answer—or so they thought. For the circumstances that were now pressing in on our "middle-class" turned "pressured-class" family were proving too much. Mom was finishing her second bout with cancer, in and out of the hospital and various forms of treatment. Dad was hanging on at work by a thread. Downsizing wasn't mixing well with all the time he spent away from work while at the hospital, or at home with us kids.

My younger brother had battles of his own. He had a mix of disorders that caused him to go up and down in a way I certainly couldn't understand—and Mom and Dad couldn't control it even had they had the time. He was on a number of meds, but there seemed to be more. I couldn't peg what it was. I knew the medical diagnosis he fought, but it was like I could explore deep into his eyes and see someone flourishing who was locked up by something he couldn't control. My heart ached for him. But in all reality, my heart ached for myself even more. Who had time for me? Where did I fit into this whole picture? I was caught in some kind of tension, like a rustling rapid without anyone there to teach me how to raft.

Up until now, the debates and commercials just approved their own ad and condemned the other. I'd hear cheering from each side of the house every now and then. But who was there to approve me, and the life I was living? I hadn't ever approved this life, and it certainly wasn't a dream. Just made me wonder, that's all.

Issues were flaring up, and hope must have been employed with Dad, because it seemed to downsize each and every year. What do you do with shrinking hope and a divided house? What do you do with politics among a divided nation? All that talking and there didn't seem like much of an answer to me. I didn't have a clue, but I did have a dream. Actually, I had quite a few. This wasn't a Martin Luther King Jr. kind of dream. No, I wasn't that radical. Plus, I was only sixteen when the dreams started. These dreams came while I slept, the only peaceful place I could find in a world without much peace to give. For a long time, I didn't want to wake up. Today, I'm writing you because I finally chose to do just that—*I chose to wake up*.

Colorado was a beautiful place to grow up. Still is. We lived in the suburbs just at the foothills of the Rocky Mountains. The peaks always overflowed into sight, even when I wasn't looking they were just trying to get noticed. It was hard to look away. Captivating. Before Mom got sick we used to take day and weekend trips up there pretty often. A lot of great memories, and a lot more hope back then. We skied, went sledding, camping, watched the aspens change in September, and went eagle watching in the late fall. To be honest, the mountains were a lot like what I wished life to be. They were tall and strong without being intimidating. They were welcoming yet held whatever amount of adventure you would ask for—a constantly present opportunity to climb higher. Covered in snow, still glistening in the sun, and they never asked for a thing—except enjoyment. To me, they were my image of hope each day, trying to buoy the spiral that I felt inside. Despite my own family's lows, I just had to look up in my heart and see the heights they still scaled.

But Colorado was also dry for me. With the altitude it is already a dry state. And it wasn't figurative for me either. The whole nation was going through a dry spell in the climate, and my life mirrored such. I was parched, and flat out celebrating any clouds I saw roll in, because even though they might come with a storm, they would also bring some rain.

My family and I already had the storms, what I was looking for was the rain to go with it. Empty clouds. That's what I call them. I was in a season of empty clouds—empty hope—and this election brought little hope, only more division. True hope usually seems to unite people. It gives you something fresh—kind of like after the rain. It's alive, new, and breathing. That's what I was longing for, to be fresh and effortlessly breathe from the inside out. No more holding my breath through divisive pressures. Hope was gasping inside my thoughts, but I needed it to breathe again, and breathe through me.

One of these days the clouds will roll in again, and despite the storm, rain will come. Every day at our home in the suburbs, no one could see through the walls or covered windows, but we were living a storm without rain. I was looking for an adventure. I wanted to climb the clouds, dodge the lightning, brace myself for the thunder and scale the skies until I personally found the rain.

I have to believe my parents wanted the same. I felt like my brother was in his own storm. And though Mom's cancer seemed to be under control, the effects it left on my parents' relationship, and the stress on the family, was far from remission. I heard too much arguing over finances, I never wanted to think about money again. My parents—in their own way—put on a pretty face for us. But to me, those masks were just more empty clouds. One thing I saw them agree on was the belief that politics would bring their answer, but they couldn't even agree on which answer that would be. It seemed like much of the nation felt the same, and social media clearly confirmed such a growing rift.

From the outside, few people would have seen the cracks in our lives. Aren't we good at covering the cracks while displaying our masks? We seem to do it so naturally that we practically project ourselves in this way as we sleep. But internally, I see our cracks. And all you show me is your mask. Doesn't make for a very nice, let alone genuine, comparison. But such is life, or so it seems. Many might look at the masks of our lives and believe we are living the dream. I'm not sure what that means. I've heard it said time and again, but do any of us really know what that dream is anymore? I mean, who's interpreting that dream, anyway?

The life my family was living was fine, I suppose—by all outward measurements. But I didn't want 'fine' anymore. I wanted hope.

I could look in the mirror and feel its reflection lying to me. Well, maybe not the mirror itself but perhaps the ways I was translating it internally. The mirror surely told me the same thing any passer by might have. By all accounts I was still the same sixteen year-old kid; wavy brown locks that my mother still loved, blue eyes I felt were growing dim and a smile that once flashed something of a curtain call, but was now left with only curtains. The mirror told my wiry frame I still had something to build off of, but I didn't feel any of the umph or strength I'd certainly need for such to be true. The truth was that I felt more like an old man at the end of my life than the fiery lad Grandpa used to call forth.

That's the reality that comes with hope dwindling away. It is not some figurative cliché, but all too real. When your hope goes, the ship seems to follow that unfortunate anchor down towards the sea creatures and fungus lying at the bottom. I didn't see myself as I was anymore—let alone as I wished to be—my lens had changed to that of an old rock collector who discovered more rough than diamonds.

All these battles were like listening for a prowler each night while I slept, hearing every creak, crack and potentially unbecoming noise that amplified themselves in the rusty turnings of my thoughts. Flopping side to side didn't help either, because truly, I didn't know what side I wanted to be on anyway. The night's approach often taunted me, making me fear I wouldn't be able to sleep, which then only became a self-fulfilling prophecy of its own.

My room was white as wool. It wasn't long ago that I covered it in posters of whatever I was passionate about in that season of my life, but the staleness in me somehow began to reflect itself in everything else too, or so it seemed. There was part of me that still wanted to redeem my surroundings, staring at the white paint that apparently was also fading to gray. So many nights I remember laying in bed, feeling tortured by any worry I could come up with, only secretly wishing my room had no ceiling, that way the stars would be in view and I could watch them puncture through the black of the night. But I couldn't even admit that much. It was a slow descent for me—eerily slow—as if I was watching myself in my own apple poisoned slumber. The lukewarm became comfortable, and then suddenly, out of nowhere, I remember even the foundation of that started to bottom out. The stars I secretly wanted to believe for were drifting even further away as I sunk further, and deeper, in fast pursuit of that sinking anchor. Until one night, without the usual struggle, but maybe a few re-directed words, I actually fell right to sleep.

That's when I started having new dreams. I had never had much religion in my family, or therefore my life. We went to a holiday service every now and then when I was a child. But we never had any prayer in our home or much interaction towards—or with—God.

However, I was at my end. As I lied down to try and wrestle myself to sleep, as I did many nights, I got desperate. The memory is still vivid like it was yesterday.

"God!" I cried out. "If you're there, if you're real, *show me something!* Take me somewhere. I NEEEEEED HOOPPPE," I lamented loudly, while hardly believing or expecting a thing.

I tossed to my other side and away from prayer, facing the wall from my bed. I half expected God to answer me in that second, and when He didn't, that was my "I told you so" kind of cold shoulder I suppose. My mind was racing with thoughts, memories—*fears*—images of my family, and all I saw going on in the world. I couldn't shut it off. Then like a sentence interrupted, I was out. Must have been fast asleep more quickly and deeply than I realized because that's when I started to dream again.

I will never forget that first dream. For that matter, I don't believe I could forget any of them. They changed me. They changed my family. Change is contagious, especially when it is motored by renewed hope. That first dream was when my hope got off life support and began a journey of its own. Hope was ready to live, and so was I.

Chapter 2:
Founder

"You may choose to look the other way but you can never say again that you did not know." - *William Wilberforce*

His name was Founder. He was large, appeared old, but was striking and incredibly regal. His presence was unlike anyone, or anything, that I had ever encountered. The first time I met him I should have been terrified, but instead, I was awestruck. He was an eagle, a bald eagle, and wisdom seemed to flow out of him like the questions circled in me. He was calm, unflinching, and his focus burned all masks, going straight to my core. I felt as if I could hide nothing from that special bird. Though, he was much more than a bird, he became my friend, my mentor, and my guide.

I feel like I'm still standing in a brisk mountain wind even now, looking on Founder's definitive features. His beak appeared as though chiseled from stone, with a golden glow that commanded attention. It was sharp, defined, and seemed to consistently point in a way that was different than I had always known—seemingly regardless of subject. He taught me a whole new way. His eyes were the warmest, wisest, most inviting portrayal of hope I had ever seen. I thought he could see for miles beyond me, and even further inside me. He called out truths and treasures from my life I never knew existed, but had always hoped for. He had a vision for my life that I longed for, a vision that he gave me. He never wrapped it in a box or with any tissue, and never asked for a thank-you. He had vision for the world that I didn't know existed, something that seemed to even be beyond hope. He was a fixture of my dreams yet felt more real than anything I could ever awake to. He opened my eyes, and then he taught me how to see.

Founder was ageless. I felt that he was long past the age any eagle should, or would, normally live to. Yet his life appeared as if it were renewed—forever young—like roots almost growing deeper rather than older. I thought wisdom must have replaced age in him. It seemed like he knew, or at least had experienced, everything. He gave you a palatable taste with his stories that were beyond knowledge or description, something that oozed off of him from genuine experience. I felt like I matured just being in his presence, but there wasn't an ounce of prestige. Pure, kind, humility marked this seemingly royal bird.

So often, I had to ask myself if he was even a bird. Founder's countenance alone showed me more than words could ever teach. He was the most genuine creature, more so than I could have ever dreamed on my own. I often wondered how such a regal, loving, wise creature could even be concocted in my dreams as I had never been around anyone or anything like him. I couldn't have imagined his qualities in the first place since it was he that brought many descriptions to life for me for the first time. He was in fact a lighthouse leading me out of stormy seas, into a new land, prepared to live a better life.

Probably the most fitting memory I have to describe him is a story he once told me about his own family. Being the face of freedom wasn't all it was cracked up to be, which is probably what qualified him to lead me in such. But politics began to rule freedom, rather than the other way around. The nation was changing, or so he said, and what is more, his family was at their own crossroads. As he recollected that part of the journey that day his eyes welled up with tears multiple times, each instance barely pushing them back down unseen, but not unfelt. I didn't mind though, it was part of the inner strength that defined my revelatory friend.

****

"Will, have I ever told you about my family?" He asked, now looking the other way.

"Of course," I answered quickly. "I know all about your great family line of eagles over this nation."

"No, Will, I mean *my family*. Have I ever told you about my mate and our one precious child? Obviously not."

"I, I'm sorry, I didn't realize…"

"How could you if I hadn't shared about them. Sometimes I lose sight of who I've shared such with. It was the pinnacle of the change I began to live out, the very change we're now walking through together. My mate, Liberty, was far stronger and wiser than I. She was absolutely radiant, and oh those piercing eyes."

He turned away again as his tears grew, almost dropping one this time.

"Liberty lived all life's possibilities before I did. Even at some of the most controversial times this nation experienced, she was the pillar strengthening the cracks in me. And at that time, I had a lot. Still do, I suppose. Liberty was about to have our first, well, our only child. We could barely hold the anticipation we felt, it was the one glimmer in our lives at a time when everything else was becoming stormy. Did you know that eagles naturally fly *towards* the storm, using them to propel even higher than before? It is innate within us not to fear such troubling times but to springboard others, and ourselves off of them. My Liberty was a true eagle. She lived what I preached and even what I faltered in. Every day she inspired me, using her words to help lift me through the storms I was to help navigate our nation through. When I would avoid the crashing lightning and thunder, she would catapult me through, and in fact over those storms as if they were never as big as they seemed, a mountain turned back into a molehill that one could easily walk on past."

"During those stormy political times, with our nation on what felt like the brink of disaster, Liberty gave me a daughter and we decided to name her Hope. She was a grizzly bear of a mom, and I was a smitten dad. As my symbol began to fade across the land, she became the star of our new family crest: *The Birth of Hope*."

"The birth of Hope may not have conquered the circumstances we were in, but was enough to light a fire under my wings so that for years to come Hope really would have a chance to freely, and abundantly, live. She was born in the late winter and Liberty was vigilant. Our little girl was the only eaglet that made it to hatch of the three, and the only little bundle of joy we would ever have. Hope, like all eaglets, grew quite rapidly, about a pound every four or five days. She was the most perfect, soft, gray I had ever laid eyes on. Most in your culture view the color gray as lacking, and empty. However, I will always see gray as a reminder of the Hope still *yet* to emerge, watching her each day become so much like her mother. I couldn't have been more proud, as you can probably tell."

"And then came the time for Hope's first attempt at flight. It's much different, Will, than when humans such as you learn to walk. Nearly half our young one's never make it through their first flight. I was terrified. I couldn't keep my nerves in place or my talons still as her first leap approached. Liberty was more confident, trusting, steady-eyed. But again, I could stare into her eyes for years at a time, they told such stories of loving perseverance."

"The day arrived for Hope's first dance with the air. She was bristling with excitement, having already visualized it at that point hundreds of times. Liberty was proud, slightly hesitant about our little eaglets venture, but still unmoved. Our nest at that time was in a towering old tree; quite worn, broken in parts, but strong where it mattered. We had nested there for years, it was such a prized location; placed on the edge of a cliff that was married to the most beautiful views creation could ask for. It was a calm wind that day, certainly not enough to be felt by those like you, Will, those who don't naturally live within the air. But the more you learn to spread your wings, the more you feel those gentle possibilities that often invisibly blow your way, always hoping you're not letting them pass by unmet."

"That moment came so fast, my little one was now perched directly in front of me and ready for her first taste of the skies. Liberty waited on a lower branch, closer to the cliff's edge. I looked down just before Hope jumped and saw my Liberty basking in the pride of that day's sun, knowing that for Hope, this was only the beginning."

Founder stepped back a little further and collapsed to the ground, letting out a wail so deep I think it has since been embedded into my soul. Even before he could continue my heart had already broke into a thousand pieces with his. While his had already been picked back up, mine were still on the mend.

"Hope leapt with such joy, Will! I want to live life with that kind of unbridled, exuberant passion. The depth of emotion in me now is only rivaled by the joy I saw in her that day. Her eyes were like her mom's, but different. While Liberty's eyes pierced the soul with her deep love and strength, Hope's told a new story, one perhaps better fit for the time she was born into, maybe even the times you're living now. Hope's eyes weren't as deeply set as her mom's—almost leaping forward—and such a physical trait wasn't lost on her spirit either; it gave those powerful new-life possibilities that were at work within her a closer edge to leap from into whoever enjoyed her company. I should know, because the story her life told leapt from that ledge into me every single day I was privileged to have her call me Papa. But that was the last day I looked into those eyes, Will, the eyes that look at you through me now are infused with my precious Hope. She flew that first dance with the wind the same way she had dreamt it every time—*freely*.

Her Mom watched as she flew downwards, passing her by, and Liberty with the very look I expected to see emblazoned across her face, the one that said, "that's my girl!" It wasn't long after that moment Liberty was able from her vantage point to see the wind was changing down below the cliff, swirling about, and Hope was daring herself too close to the cliff's rocky exterior and extended branches. All it took was one gust to knock her into a protruding, rugged edge, and Hope's leap turned from flying to unconsciously falling. Liberty dove after her before I even knew what was happening. Before I could actually see the danger at hand, or do anything about it, Liberty was already in a determined dive halfway down the cliff, chasing Hope. Chasing Hope in that moment became a mission, a way of life that was such a natural part of Liberty, she couldn't have kept on living without going head-first after our girl."

"I dove down myself, but was far too late, just entering perspective to see their fall unfold, myself already half-way dying inside. Liberty caught her, with the swiftest swoop I'd ever witnessed, but with no time to avoid the iced over, boulder ridden river below. Liberty died too, with Hope in her grasp. I lost my girls that day, and nothing hurts worse, nor will anything ever grip my heart in such a way."

I wiped the streaming tears from my face, feeling every moment he described. I already felt like I knew them both.

"I wish you could have, Will." He answered quickly. "I wish you could have known them. But, in a sense, you do. I lost Liberty too early, and truly, in every sense imaginable, my Hope was gone too. They were the deepest, most painful, but life-giving scars I ever endured. My heart eventually healed, and those scars are now why I have so much Liberty every day, and why I will never cease to let Hope live through me. She's the one with the story to tell, she's the one who revived my old, broken and bitter soul. I lost Liberty, and Hope, but they helped find me. And now they lead me to know those like you. I will never let Hope, or Liberty, die again."

****

Much of that story rang loudly throughout my many adventures with Founder. It's the one I always tell first, because it told me so much, not only about his life, but why he has meant so much to mine. From the first time I met Founder, whether I knew it yet or not, Liberty and Hope were written across every part of him, practically glowing through his features and emboldening his heart, trying to live again, and looking for those who would still allow them to. I wish you could know him like I did. And, maybe you can.

Founder lived adventure as if they weren't adventures at all. It was life. He led me on paths and met me in places that will never be the same. I will never be the same because of this splendid eagle, who spread his wings and opened my eyes. That reminds me—*his wings*—they were like every hug I had always wanted that seemed out of reach. Without even a touch I could feel his wings around me, under me, over me, and giving me flight. The rustic bronze of his feathers uniquely reflected the sun, and made me feel like a son. I know that might sound odd—*a child of an eagle?* But the truth was, that's how I felt. I was given new life! I was…*made new.* His wings revealed more about the world than I had ever known from within the walls of our house or the patterns of our life. The greatest ups of our family had never taught me what his scars could. Just looking upon those scars on his wings, each healed wound, was like a journey to venture into with more adventure waiting to become my own experience. We didn't have to go anywhere to take in new life, I found new life in him. Or perhaps he found it in me.

Founder's talons are a memory I still feel while awake. Even now, as I write our story, I can feel him gripping my shoulder gently as if he were right here helping me recount my new hope tale. He had carried me with those talons and lifted me above the confusion I so easily could have fallen further into. He propelled me from my dry storms through a wind trending upwards, a vortex of seemingly ridiculous possibilities. With

21

Founder, I didn't just dream, he taught me to go even higher.

Eagles are known for the heights they soar to. They are known to mount the skies as the chariot they ride. Founder's height became my new vision of hope. He helped me scale my own internal mountains so that I could see from their peaks. I tasted such a high that I soon found out for myself, as I watched them float by, that truly no cloud is in the slightest bit empty. Now, I got to taste rain without the storms. Isn't that a nice turnaround? And little did my family know that Founder was actually the pioneer of the new joy that took hold of our family—for the very first time.

The first time we met wasn't in a cloud or what you would think a dream world might be. It was all too unique. Founder and I met at the zoo. Well, it wasn't a real zoo, but it was the first place I met him in my dreams—more on that in a minute. I know what you must be thinking, or asking—*a zoo?* I had the same questions. How could such a regal, wise bird come from a zoo? While he certainly didn't come *from* there, it was the first place he and I had such an encounter. I probably would have thought the same as you. I would have expected something, or somewhere, that was far more exotic. But, you would have to know Founder. He sees a lot differently than most of us do, almost inside out, and he knew exactly where to find me. Through those fresh eyes of his my sinking perspective became a multi-faceted diamond, where so much more of life could be appreciated through a different glare.

He introduced me to friends everywhere. Each one held a story or unique piece of life and light that I didn't even recognize inside myself as needing to be quenched. And together, Founder and I faced what I now know to be the greatest enemy of all.

Chapter 3:
The First Dream:
In The Enclosure

"It is difficult to free fools from the chains they revere."
- Voltaire

I've been to the zoo many times, but this wasn't like any of them. I was in an enclosure, and there were sheep all around me. There were no bars blocking my escape, just a deep cavern all around the edges with large rocks and bushes piled up one on top of the other. Natural life flowed through the cracks of a nature that man built. I could probably get out if I wanted to, but I didn't feel all that threatened by the sheep that were surrounding me. At first thought, I was just thankful be amid such docile

24

creatures, compared to the hidden roars that had to be just around the corner. The sheep were on all sides of me, kind of odd to tell you the truth. I was sitting in the middle of the enclosure on a smooth, medium sized boulder, no bigger than your average kitchen table. The typical noises of the zoo were oddly missing; at least the sounds zoo goers usually create during open hours, as no one else was in sight. The only sounds I heard were these unheralded sheep, the lions boasting in the background, birds each making their own unique squawk and squeal, wolves howling like the moon was out, and hyenas cackling unmercifully with laughter; laughter that would have been a welcome addition to my family's home on any given day, but was currently riding my patience. There were no kids calling for their parents while running ahead to the next exhibit. No hungry, crying babies or any of the typical chatter that constitutes your typical public white noise of such a park.

It was the middle of the day judging by the sun, and the world almost felt frozen, except for these grappling sheep just before me. The sheep interacted in an unusual way. Not that I was any expert on sheep or anything, having seen them only a few times in my life. But something was odd. Although, being in the middle of a zoo enclosure was pretty odd itself, so I suppose it was a fitting dream for me after all, as perplexing, nonsensical dreams were usually the language of the night during this confusing time in my life. Despite the unusual circumstances, to be honest, I was getting a little bored. I mean, what was I supposed to do living in a sheep's world? But suddenly, my focus wasn't on them anymore. A giant eagle swooped onto the scene.

It glided into my sight with its wings open, fanning wildly for its landing. There were no air traffic controllers waving him in, though with the size of it you sure would have thought there could have been. The overwhelming bird landed swiftly and precisely, taking residence at the top of a long, upward slanted beam of wood that was resting on a mound of scraps just in front of me. It would have been startling, being only a few feet away and all, if it didn't carry such an unusual peace. I had never spent much time with animals, let alone birds. We had gone camping—even eagle watching—but rarely got even remotely close. And we never had any interaction. Can't imagine that many people do.

When it first landed, it just stared at me. But it wasn't in an intimidating way. The only words that can explain it is a mixture of curiosity and, well, love. It caught me off guard, though which part I couldn't figure out. But by love, I mean that the eagle took a genuine interest, like it was coming to me with purpose, and in a way that made it seem like it really cared, and almost seemed worried. He was defined by goodness, which seemed to welcome my trust before I could even hesitate to hand it over.

"What are you doing here?" he belted out with more than an ounce of concern, which took me completely by surprise. I lost the concern while I searched for understanding. My mouth was agape and I couldn't pick it back up.

"What?" I responded briskly. "Did you say something?" I asked not even remembering what he spoke, just trying to figure out if this eagle was truly talking to me.

He moved beyond my apparent disrespect, shaking his head with ruffled feathers, but once again through a deep, raspy, but softened voice he asked, *"What are you doing here?"*

I had to stop and ask myself that question internally a few times before I could gather myself to answer. I was still a little shell-shocked to be conversing with a bird, to tell you the truth.

"What do you mean, what am I doing here? Where am I? I don't know where I am, let alone what I'm doing here—except for the fact that this is some kind of zoo and apparently I am hanging out here with these sheep," I answered with a half grin. I think I was more amused than anything else.

"Sheep?" he responded strongly. His eyes took on an entirely different look while his feathers bristled wildly. "What sheep are you talking about?" The eagle asked in an increasingly disturbed way. "Yes, this is indeed a zoo, but those are not sheep. You should not be here, it isn't safe at all." The eagle looked nervous, but not for himself.

He very obviously knew something I didn't.

"What do you mean these aren't sheep? I think I have seen enough sheep in my life to recognize one pretty easily. They're harmless."

Barely finishing my statement, and faster than the eagle had swooped in and landed near me, the closest sheep fiercely lunged right at me. In the same breath, almost as if he knew the danger we were in, the eagle scooped me with his talons into the air in what felt like an impossible task and looped us out of the enclosure just beyond the trenches and onto a viewing bench. As we landed, I was shaking from head to toe, and had no idea what was taking place. At the same time I heard a chorus of loud howls as I locked eye-to-eye with this spectacle of a wild bird. He was royal in his definition, and poignant in a character that bled from him freely, naturally commanding my attention like the most respected of leaders.

"Those are not sheep," he said again, this time with an exhausted emphasis. "Those are wolves. Why were you there? And why in the world would you think they were sheep?" he asked with an urgent, almost fatherly tone.

"Wolves? I didn't see any wolves. I heard wolves, but I assumed they were much farther away in a different sector of the zoo. I saw nothing but sheep, nor anything else to make me believe otherwise. And still, I don't know how I got here in the first place."

"Did you really not know that those were wolves?" He asked again while considering my apparent ignorance.

"I had no idea," I answered, shaking my head, a little more nervous and taken back than before.

"Then I know why you are now here," the eagle said pointedly, exhaling a deep breath while regaining great clarity and focus. My eyes grew bigger just hearing his answer.

"You do? Then why?" I asked.

"If you could not see the wolves for the sheep, I venture to say you have come here on purpose—for the sake of your dreams. I am your guide. My name is Founder. I will explain more as we go."

I wanted to be leery of what he was saying, but something deep inside me—something I hadn't heard make a peep for years—was begging me to listen. Founder seemed to present the opportunity I was looking for in life, perhaps just in a much different package than I expected. And, I was still trying to realize the danger he had just kept me from. He lifted up off the bench and motioned towards me with a nod of his head and the pointing of his beak; "Follow me."

He led me farther along the path we walked on, around the very same enclosure I had found myself sitting in previously. We went up a slight, leading hill, past a sign that read "Bird's Eye View," and onto a bridge overlooking the shee...um...I guess, I mean the wolf enclosure. I had heard the term "a wolf in sheep's clothing" before, many times, but it was clear this case was much more than a familiar phrase. And now, I could watch for myself as this fable unfolded before my eyes. I looked down on the pack of howling wolves licking their chops, looking up at us, undeterred and salivating, clearly recognizing, maybe even targeting me from before.

And to top it off there wasn't one sheep in sight. The boulder I had been sitting on now looked more like a breakfast table, covered in old scraps and drippings. I felt the gulp dropping through my throat and chest like a crashing temperature, while my mind raced through fear after fear. I felt I must be about as stark white as Founder's head feathers. Now I was really confused, and frightened too. I turned to look at the large eagle for comfort, and he looked back at me like he knew my every thought, while seeking to quench every fear. For that alone I was thankful.

Founder's eyes went straight past my gaze and down to my heart and soul. Looking into his vision I now knew something I didn't know how to put words to, something I couldn't have known before. Something was planted inside me like a seed from his stare. His vision told the whole story, or perhaps at that moment, just the beginning of it, but it was enough. He looked at me differently than anyone had before, with a passionate urgency that urged me to see and know something, like he believed in me. But, I didn't know why.

The seed inside me told me why he was there, why I was there—to help me with what it means to *truly see*, because in that moment, my eyes were opened to a rare world that blind spots couldn't accompany me to. This dream was alive, and now through the sight of those wolves it revealed what I had long been suspicious of— much of my life up to this point had been a lie. Apparently, I was in a dream, and that dream was already reinterpreting my life.

"Many who do not see the wolves here are missing out on many of the wolves there," Founder said delicately, referring, I believe, to my life while awake. "And if you are missing the wolves, then you are certainly missing out on much of what those wolves are secretly stealing from you; life they are devouring, the hope that is possible, and the dreams that could still be before you; which they are clearly snatching from you before you can even fall asleep. The wolves are a hidden enemy disguised within normal culture. They are keepers of the box you must be free to break out of. Any good, deceptive box is like that enclosure you sat within; a man made version of what could be natural. There's no freedom in that."

There was still a small part of me that wanted to hesitate to listen or believe such tales, or to engage this unique reality, but still, there was a huge pull inside me that was more and more drawn to Founder, like I had been unknowingly waiting to hear what he was speaking out. I didn't have to cognitively understand yet, because something inside me knew exactly what language he was speaking, and that was a culture I wanted to be part of. Founder and his words were proving to be the picture my heart truly wanted. I felt he knew a different kind of hope, something both old and new at the same time.

We were still standing up on the bridge overlooking the wolf enclosure and something was very much amiss to me. *Why did I think they were sheep?* Why wouldn't I just see nothing if I couldn't see the wolves? Founder must have been reading my mail or something, because he began answering my questions before I could even ask them.

"The sheep are a false sense of security, and a watered down dream. Much like when someone 'counts sheep' to help lull themselves off to sleep, the sheep represent the things or parts of culture not often questioned, ways that become the norm—comfortable ways—which many simply conform to. You see them because a part of you wants to see them. It is normal to become like our surroundings and ignore the vision that's living inside of us."

"The wolves of culture will rarely attack you unless you present a threat to understanding your greater purpose, which is why one lunged for you down there when he saw you with me. They typically don't go for the jugular of hope like that. No, they are far too smart for such, then everyone would know the hidden enemy they are. Instead, they take your hope like sheep led to slaughter, presenting lies to a few, knowing that most will follow the pack. They know you will lead one another astray. Most people lose their vision for true purpose and begin to live the life of a sheep. The wolves of culture know this and are a far greater enemy than many of the more obvious enemies you face in the world. They are deceptive and fabricate a lie of comfort, and therefore conformity. They are like the old parable of the frog and the pot of water. If you put a frog into a boiling pot of water, it will immediately jump out. But if you put a frog in a lukewarm pot of water and gradually turn up the heat, the frog will allow itself to be boiled and served because it became a sheep, following the comfort of its lukewarm surroundings. I am here, Will, to awaken your vision and help you dream, again. I have been peering in on your life for some time now, not knowing when our season together would come, and I want to answer that thirst for true hope you have inside. Don't ever let that be quenched, for your thirst is the thing those wolves want most."

While I had other questions, I had to ask him. "How did you know my name?"

"Will, like I said, I have been watching you for some time now. I have seen your potential and I am here because of the truth of that potential inside you. You have been looking for refreshed hope, praying for it even. Well, Will, that hope is seemingly hidden, but inherent within you."

I saw the gleam in Founder's eye as he spoke that last part. I think it must have activated a spark in my own. I could feel the hope of hope arising in me like I too could begin to fly. But I still didn't have wings, even though my goose bumps told me otherwise.

"You will get your wings soon enough, dear Will, soon enough.

****

I remember clearly how I felt waking up from that first dream. I was a little caught off guard to say the least, but I must have caught something because I hadn't felt that alive, or more awake, in years. One of the first things I did when I awoke was look down for wings, as if I suddenly had the capacity to fly. I suppose I was a little too caught up. My senses were heightened and nothing felt impossible. That is, until I went downstairs and joined those who were still treading water in the same reality that I wished to be transformed.

I loved my family, I really did. And still do. But their lack of hope back then, compared with what I had received from Founder that first dream, was terribly contagious in the opposite and what felt like the most harmful of ways. Hope deferred had truly made our hearts grow sick. And that dream had become my new medicine. Finally, I had been able to see it for myself. They were sheep too. That meant our house had become a culture of wolves. Founder was right. I needed new eyes. And I couldn't wait to dream, again.

Chapter 4:
The Second Dream:
Ridge of Hope

"It's not what you look at that matters, it's what you see."
- Henry David Thoreau

Founder and I were on a ridge so high that it didn't feel like we were on the ground anymore at all. His talons gripped a large, fallen tree branch. My own feet gripped the edge of the mountain, which unfortunately felt about as shaky as my grip on life. The ridge was one of the highest skylines among the Colorado mountain ranges I often looked up to from our front yard.

I always enjoyed the view of the mountains, longing

for what they had to offer. But now more than any sight of them ever before I was overwhelmed not just by the powerful presentation they offered, but by my perspective *from* them. The possibilities they so confidently declared made me teeter between fear of falling from their ledge and standing firm to take in the increase their perspective freely gave. I couldn't decide which one to believe. Fear seemed to have its usual comforts and safe ending, but I was now beginning to realize that the path of fear so often seems to lead to easy comfort. Hope is what I needed, but fear had a megaphone in my mind, telling me how risky it perceived my new posture to be. So, I turned off the power supply I too frequently funded, the part of me that allowed fear's voice to be heard. There had been too much barking of orders for far too long in my life, too many self-imposed limits. I was ripe for a new coach in my life, not another whistle-blowing referee.

I could see for miles in every direction. There wasn't anything tall enough to block my way. The air and view was a culture of its own; thin enough to fly higher, broad enough to drift out and explore. Founder sat in silence while I took it all in, like he didn't need to say a thing. And truly, he probably didn't. I was learning already, much more than words I was seeing from a higher place. My body was trembling, but not nearly as much as my heart.

It was interesting to feel the tightrope of fear and hope that my feet were still curled around, the life I wanted being teased by the taunts of slipping alone at the simple expense of truly living. Every moment I chose perspective over fear, I gained something that is beyond what I can describe. I had looked at these mountains so often, but seeing them only for what I was ready to digest. I never knew what they could see, or what more they wanted to feed me. But I had never asked either. I realized that if an eagle such as Founder could speak, I figured the mountains must be able to as well. And yet, I felt I hadn't even scratched the surface judging by the palpitations of my heart. Purple mountains majesty was a song making its way deep past the echo on my lips, and into the reality my spirit wanted to prove true.

My mind was spinning while it searched to understand all I was taking in, like learning a new language amidst the streets of a new culture. I had no words or understanding to speak to the language that my eyes were showing me. It became clear that this silent sight of perspective was the dialect of these high up peaks. It really was like seeing for the very first time— except when I looked down of course, I'd too often seen that spiral and the perilous comforts fear offered. That was the sight of fear, self and circumstances; views that were all too familiar that I had clearly allowed to dictate, or rather steal, far too much of my hope. When I looked up and out, I flourished, learned and had new hope that couldn't even begin to be contained. When I looked down, I immediately felt paralyzed and wondered why I would even think about being in such a place. Wow! I was amazed such a subtle difference could create such a stark contrast. They were powerful waves colliding inside me, and I was learning to surf those swells of confusion and doubt that tried to intimidate me.

Founder sat nearby with a sheepish grin on his face, if that's what an eagle's grin looks like anyway. Perhaps sheepish wasn't the right word though, I thought with half a laugh, and no more. He had a smirk like I used to see on Grandpa when he was all too tickled with himself. The smirk of this bird spoke loudly at the moment, almost as loudly as my eyes could see. And probably louder than anything he could say.

"What you are perceiving is a view that has been there the entire time. This is the *Ridge of Hope*. It is a peek into a different life that is available to all. Perspective such as this feeds your vision for life. Your eyes can only process what they can see directly in front of them, which is why so many struggle; they live by what the wolves of the world present. True vision leads you into more than words or circumstance can describe, presenting a new, fresh buffet of hope. New perspective is a necessary ingredient for hope to breathe again. You have to see what the wolves don't want you to see, rather than take what they freely offer. They cannot take what you don't give them."

"You have been living in a culture of wolves that lure sheep into a counterfeit vision, where conformity is celebrated by seeing who can be the most successful sheep. It appears as a ladder of success, but is actually the upside down spiral that fear dictates. Such is the pride that wars against vision. True vision comes from a higher peak of perspective, such as this. It keeps you hungry and thirsty because you see that there is actually more available than the world's gift-wrapped box may present. It is a hope that never stops growing. Hope is not the end that you seek, it is the means to re-discover the truth that waits hidden and buried by those wolves underground. It's the path that pioneers a different, unchartered way through the packs and herds the wolves will make sure you are always surrounded and pressured by. The wolves want you to rely on sight because then they get to control what you see. But when you take back vision for your life, you will be dictating to them a life that grows the other direction, a life they are most afraid of, unearthing that which they have tried to steal and bury."

"Will, fear and pride work together to keep you on their treadmill, they are the whip and the whistle that hold the pack of sheep in herd. Pride keeps you measuring and protecting yourself while living up to the other sheep, and fear keeps you from looking up and stepping into the life this perspective can show you. The genuine battle of fear and hope you feel while both standing and seeing from this ridge only reminds you that you are once again at a crossroads of choice. Vision is widely available, but it will not force itself upon you, it's something you must always pursue, never allowing your hunger for such hope to be quenched. At the same time, you will hear the quietly intimidating whispers of fear sneaking up your thoughts as if they were the ground's own roots growing up your legs, seeking to pull you back down. I have seen it far too many times. No matter what, you have to believe before you can truly see. This will always be the case. And Will, I believe in you."

"Also, remember, to be in this place does not mean you have arrived at the top of the mountain. Rather, this is where your new journey begins, *from* the top of the mountain. You are at the intersection of past cycles and hope reformed. This is the place where you yourself must choose. Will you journey forward with this new vision available all around you, waiting to be seized? Or through the comfortable cycle rounding back down to the bottom of the mountain where there is little fear of falling, only that of being slowly boiled like the frog in the kettle? Will, I can't guide you any further into this choice, I can only ask you, *what do you see?*"

I didn't know how to answer. I knew what I wanted to answer. As much as I wanted hope, I wanted the perspective and different life that this peak portrayed. But it wasn't that simple, or that easy. I could practically see the sheep of such wolf culture at the bottom only waiting for me to return, expecting it actually, and oh how I wanted to prove them wrong. But fear of falling almost made me want to walk straight back into the insurance and security the pack of sheep seemed to provide. If I wasn't supposed to be a sheep, what was I?

"That is precisely what I was trying to ask you," Founder interjected. "I was not asking you yet, what you see out there," he said while motioning his wing out and around. "I was asking you what you see—right there?" he said quietly while nodding his head with an emphasis toward my heart. "Do you want to be a sheep led by wolves, or, who are you?"

That question opened up a flood of questions that didn't seem possible on such a high mountain. It made me look inside. As much as I clearly wanted to state that I was no sheep, I had to question myself, just as I had not known those original sheep were actually wolves. Might I have been seeing myself as more free than I was actually living? Was I ever really that different from a sheep being led by a wolf culture? It made me think round and again of my past and my family, places and thoughts I was only just beginning to lift away from. I clearly knew I needed to see well enough to break away from the pack.

I started to sink into my thoughts and memories, which blurred my newfound vision from this ridge. I think Founder saw the drain my thoughts had me spiraling towards as he tried to interrupt.

"Will…Will! Can you hear me? Listen!" Founder yelled, but it sounded like a whisper to me. "Will, be careful, your past is not a place to go for answers to this question. You can learn from your past, but must not be defined by it. It is like quicksand, or a trance from a false, lying reality. I am not asking you what anyone or any circumstance says. Other sheep cannot make you a sheep unless you follow them in place of something greater. That vision can only come from you. Vision can go deep into the pits of our past and see well enough not just to climb out, but flourish again. Will, what do *you* see?"

"I…uh, I, I don't know. I don't know what I see. Isn't that what you are here for?"

"Will, I am only your guide. I cannot see for you. I am here to show you a different way, to highlight an unseen truth, and to help you choose a better life. But I cannot do that for you. There is much more power when it comes from what you choose. I once went through my own crises of vision."

I looked back at Founder with a bewildered look.

"Huh?" I responded with clarity and sophistication, as always.

"You see, Will, to an eagle, vision is one of the most natural components of life. But it is easy to allow familiarity to rob our greatest places of joy and strength. For a time, I stopped coming to places such as this because I thought I had seen all they had to offer. I forgot that the perspective up here means nothing if I don't open my eyes to receive what is freshly present. Not to mention what started such an epidemic. People. Well, perhaps they were sheep in some ways. But no matter what, they weren't the problem. I was. I allowed them to lead me astray from a strength that is so innate to my nature."

"I had my own experience at a zoo much like the one where we recently met. Well, I had many experiences there that perhaps one day I will share with you in detail. But this one in particular always sticks in my mind; *it changed me*. My father, a strong, prominent eagle was fulfilling his family calling. My mother and I had been taken captive by researchers who placed us under watch in a zoo. There were bars, glass and netting all around. Mom couldn't see well anymore but I don't think any of the onlookers knew that. Her blindness was actually a strength at that time, it caused her to see with eyes different than everyone else's, mine included."

"Every day people came by to get a look, and they all thought they knew us. They had their own opinions, their jokes and insults, their own reason for idolizing us, and then they would move on. But you know what, Will? I couldn't. I couldn't move on. I tried so hard to prove them wrong, in my own ways of course, that I didn't actually realize that by fighting for their perspective of me I was really proving them right. If I truly knew who I was and had clear vision inside me, then I wouldn't need to prove a thing to anyone. I would just know. The more I listened to the onlookers who didn't even know me the more I changed to become less like me. Well, my vision changed. And once my vision changed, that's what changed me for a time."

"It was a difficult time in my life. Every day I found my worth—or lack thereof—through the eyes of those who were passing by and I lost the true vision that was already a treasure deep inside. It took some time to recover from that season in life. Even more, it took some time to fully realize that those wounds weren't from any of the onlookers at all, but were actually self-inflicted."

"See, Will, even an eagle can lose its vision. But Mom, oh, she was fine. Like I said, the blindness seemed to work in her favor. She was as jovial as ever, totally unaware of the perspective of others because her own eyes weren't her measure. No, she had to rely on knowing who she was without the reflection of a mirror or of the people. The only eyes she had left to see with were those that were firmly planted and joyfully alive on the inside. She lived and finished a most splendid life because of such vision. Sure, she bumped into things here and there and people laughed, but what did she care? You don't have to worry so much about where you are going when you first know who you are."

"That is how you must learn to see yourself, Will. You cannot look for a hopeful future if you continue to place your hope in other people's eyes. Just as you will never realize a future any other than what the wolves put on your plate if you use the rearview mirror as your primary lens. You can look in the mirror a thousand times and always see something, and maybe even *someone* different, someone brimming with new life and natural smiles. Or, you can look in the mirror a thousand times and see the same someone who you think is simply drying up into a statue of what was, or what could have been. In fact, I think I should have rephrased my question to you in the first place. Realize this, what you see is important, but it cannot come until you can answer the lens of *how* you see. What is it that dictates, shades, clouds or gives light to the vision of *who* you are?"

"Perhaps I moved too fast for you before, Will, I'm sorry about that," Founder said with new resolve. "I want to take this at your pace, because this is your journey and will have much further reaching impact than you yet know. The process is far more important than just the destination. Your journey is your own, and it is not bound to time. It is not bound to anyone else's journey, even my own. I don't want you to try and define yourself until you've learned to see differently. So before we go back to seeing you, let's start with something else. Look up—*out there*—and tell me, what do you see?"

Founder directed my attention towards the east. It overlooked the Front Range, the very suburbs I came from. But I had never seen it quite like this before. It's amazing how familiarity really does blind us. There was a glow of possibility over the region below us, but just under that hopeful glow a musky smog permeated up and down, like it was trying to smother the light, while also seeping down like a freshly painted, dripping ceiling over the neighborhoods—fumes and all. Among the sunlight and smog, there was nothing new. But seeing—and thinking—about them from this perspective made them look more like a metaphor, revealing much of the battle I was trying to win where I'd push through the smog to what is up here, now seeing from the other side.

The smog was manmade from culture, but the light was everlasting, and natural. They were two cultures clearly colliding and I was trying to learn which one to live by. One came easily, but the other, well, it should come naturally. It had not been natural for ages, if ever for me. Perhaps it had been too long for many others as well. It's amazing the sentences the horizon could speak, and so effectively. And down beneath the cloudy smog in the culture of wolves were millions of sheep. Was I still one of them?

Founder began to guide my vision elsewhere, leading my sight clockwise to the south, then the west, and finally up north. Amazing what a different view and culture each direction possessed seeing from a lighthouse like this. All of them were similarly alive, a stark contrast to the front-range that was but a handful of cities, supposed to be most alive, suburbs and where we usually find "the dream life." Each of these other views showed me a natural perspective of a culture less tainted by the wolves and aspiring sheep, a culture that still seemed at least a little ripe for dreaming.

"What do you see?" Founder asked again.

"Honestly, I don't know if I can do it justice. But more than anything, I suppose, I see....possibility! I see hidden, untapped potential waiting to be explored in new ways. I see life that grows to the north, south, and west. To the east, I see a life that that seems to be a statue of its former self. I can't see the horizon there anymore because of all the smog."

"You're seeing well, dear boy. Perspective is doing you wonders already," Founder stated with a sturdy nod. "Do you see a bridge?" he asked, without any curiosity at all, obviously a rhetorical question. I knew the answer he was looking for. But the truth of the matter is that I could see no bridge, and didn't want to speak what I knew to be the right answer at the expense of truly learning the right one.

"No, I don't," I answered frankly.

Look again," Founder said.

I have to admit, I was a little frustrated. I wanted desperately to learn, I really did, but honestly, I wanted Founder to simply give me a few of the answers.

"That's the sheep in you," Founder interrupted my thoughts.

"What?" I furrowed my brow at him, allowing a little of the teenager back out of me I suppose. "I'm sorry, Founder. What I meant was; what do you mean?" He answered me quickly and pointedly.

"*Sheep want answers.* But you, you are created to live your answers. Create them! Let them out of you. Fly higher! So, Will, look again. Do you see a bridge between the differences and the possibilities?"

I buckled down in my mind, determined to think differently. Bridge? What bridge, I questioned, asking myself this time. We must have stood there in silence for what seemed like an hour, though it was probably closer to ten minutes. I stared from the ridge we were on into the east, gazing down over the area my own house would be found. I was lost in thought without flinching, diving deeper into the expanding deep end of my own thoughts and perspective in ways I never would have before. It felt good, refreshing, like my eyes were indeed opening just a little bit wider. I could tell I was re-modeling my own thinking with every new thought.

"I got it! I got it!" I blurted out, with a spring in my step and no regard for the edge that was so nearby. "*I am the bridge!* My vision, my perspective, they are a bridge from here to there. I am the bridge between the two sides and the war of cultures. The bridge is in me and how I choose to see, right? Like a rainbow of perspective ready to be walked on, a pot of previously hidden gold sure to be awaiting." I stated with startling enthusiasm, far beyond actually asking a question.

My favored eagle friend looked down upon me with pride in his eyes. "There is a lot to be found in your own choosing, isn't there Will? Your vision holds a lot more power than you thought. Your vision and how you live it out truly is a bridge where sheep can escape from the ways of the wolves and be led once again on a path of promise, as you said, like walking on a rainbow that transcends the light, *and the storm*, which collide to bring that bridge to life."

"Most people are waiting for answers, rather than choosing to *be* an answer. Will, you are a bridge for your own family, and so many others who need the vision you are now learning. Your life is a bridge from this peak of hope to the pastures the sheep are trying to live in. But before any bridge can be walked on, its own foundations must be strengthened. There are many nuts and bolts you don't have yet. There is an engineering process your perspective is going through to renew your mind and transform you into a bridge of limitless hope. The renewing of your mind and thoughts empowers you to re-dream the American dream, and therefore remodel the possibilities that lie before you and so many others. It's not an easy journey, and it hardly seems natural anymore to those where you are from. However, such a journey will unlock the hidden dream within you that is bigger than anything anyone else has ever dreamed for you, bigger than what any wolf can carry off with its teeth. Is this a journey you wish to venture into further? I promise you, it won't be easy. I promise you, there are adventures waiting to be had. I promise you, it will hurt. And I promise you, Will, that I will be your guide the whole way."

Was there really anything else to say except for yes? Founder stood resolutely, looking into my eyes with almost uncomfortable depth from his. How far into me could he see? As uncomfortable, and almost culturally violating as it seemed, it was a welcome housecleaning as well. I trusted this endearing eagle. He brought out answers in me that I didn't even have a question for yet. And I could only imagine how many more unknown questions were waiting inside me to be asked.

Chapter 5:
Meanwhile: The Wolf Culture

"I am enough of an artist to draw freely upon my imagination. Imagination is more important than knowledge. Knowledge is limited. Imagination encircles the world." - *Albert Einstein*

With well-disguised lies us wolves carried on in our ways. Most avoid our dens to make way from the wolves, but the most dangerous of wolves don't actually live in dens, "Do they, Son?"

"No, Father, as you've told me many times, our culture has only lived to be one for the ages, and we'll only continue to live that way, as long as we lie in the less obvious places, holing up in the minds of men."

This old eerie factory had become our primary place of residence, manufacturing deception the way others produce bubble gum—trying to give everyone something of ours to chew on I suppose. Like most days, I could feel that edge lingering about the premises. It was the pheromones I suppose coming from the uncontrollable dripping of my fangs. I, however, wasn't primed to bite, no, I possessed a far greater appetite now than what my mouth, or stomach, could easily hold. My taste buds enjoyed the wild, gamey tastes of free culture, and growing my following. I had to carry such a presence, as lies require intimidation, or what most just refer to as the pressures of the world. Yep, the room was loaded as usual while all my fellow species followed my orders, err, I mean, my leadership, like sheep. But they liked it this way, at least now they did. Wolves typically travel in packs, but I've learned to prefer the herd mentality myself.

As my cub, Skotos, looked at me with unadulterated loyalty, not knowing the deception he was raised in, I couldn't help but beam with pride. I know a pride is supposed to be what the lions travel in, but I've become quite taken by such myself. "Lies and self," I declared out loud, "that's how we burrow into the minds of men."

"But Dad, what do you mean, lies? What lies? This is the only truth I've ever known."

"Precisely, Skotos, and that's exactly what many

more each year have come to say," I smiled gleefully. "I'm all sheep to you, and you will always be my little lamb. The more we make them sheep, we'll just use our wool to cover their eyes and blend right in to the culture of freedom they call their own. We'll be the sheep they elect for office, and the one's who quietly pressure their fear. We'll feed them all they can handle until the freedom to eat of the world consumes their dreams. See, when they feed self, essentially, they feed us. Like fattening a Christmas pig, we wait until the opportune time to devour what they feed themselves right now. The more they feed self they actually become active participants in giving their lives away—not a sacrifice for noble cause, however—rather, they feed our dream instead. When they feed self, they position themselves for the slaughter we personally await. They lose sight of the dream their heart was created to beat for and all they can do is fill up the belly that will one day, feed us. We could never get them to our dens; as such tactic has been tried and discovered too many a times. Sure, many wolves have still gotten their share of sheep, but our culture is in it for the long haul. We too have learned from other wolves' mistakes. We don't hide under red capes anymore nor seek to blow a house down; our deception has deepened with time, just as you said, becoming the only truth known.

We don't have to attack nearly as often when we can lead so many of them willingly to slaughter. I mean, have you ever considered debt. I know, it doesn't sound like a very prolific, new plan, but it works. We build billboards of expectation to strive for, and debt is usually the only way to measure up to the seemingly harmless and necessary standards we set. Debt is like a conveyor belt, whether it be for a person, a culture, or a nation; a conveyor belt that eventually leads right to our table. I don't need to slaughter sheep that are putting themselves on our factory line, leading one another to slaughter. These are the ways we've deceived so many for ages, but we've begun to up our ante. Now, it's the ways we plan to lead them. They've given over enough of their dreams as collateral, they have very little left but us, once they see us as their only hope that is."

"But Dad, what if they don't elect one of our sheep? What if they don't rely on the election at all? What...what if, if they find their wings again?"

"It's a great question, Son, but easier said then done. We've given most of them just enough not to go looking for what they've lost. We've spoon fed their freedom, turned their wings into monuments of man made stone with no quality of life whatsoever, and we've turned their dreams into using their precious houses, bank accounts and white picket fences to protect the little we've allowed them to keep. And the few who have, or will figure it out, they'll sound like lunatics to the rest, crazy people spouting off on street corners at best. And just in case, we have plenty of our "plants" on the inside that are actually using old school, wolf tactics to feed the bigger model of the new of course. They can spin anything into our taste of propaganda, and they know how to remove any DNA ridden saliva we may just so happen to leave behind. Skotos, one day not too far from now they will all have as much faith in these truths as you have. That is the day I am waiting for. We just need to keep going about our business, watch the lies feed self, and self, well, watch self feed us!" I couldn't help but laugh, and even better to have my own offspring join in the riot. There wasn't much left to do. Well, but for one thing.

"Have you heard the phrase, 'Hope deferred makes the heart grow sick?' Well, we've made it our culture's mission statement. Every hope we can defer, deflecting it out of one's heart and onto a circumstance, that gives us access to that point of said heart. When hope becomes external, we can crush it through all the other measures we already have in place. Hope is clearly an inside job. If one leans on positive circumstance to gird up their hope, we have them right where we want them. It's a slow, step-by-step process to not be noticed, but it's worked so far. Essentially, when we get hope on the outside we get the sheep begging for hope from us, which is exactly what we're after. And in the meantime, piece-by-piece of heart after heart is growing dimly ill, fattened with hurt and doused with bitterness. The heart begins to hate the very thing that can help it, an elixir of life already available within. When hope is deferred, as I said, the heart grows sick. When the heart grows sick, well, it turns into stone, just like the other monuments that were once life-giving movements of multiplication. At this point, there is only one way to address such glorious results, a new heart and a new spirit. But thankfully, that's exactly what most cast away once their hope is deferred. And the whole process is really quite easy to launch, all we must do is bait their hope to be in the costly lies we've created on the outside, a false freedom, rather than allowing them to see and therefore access all that could be freely available within. That lie is a devourer by itself, among the greatest seeds our culture has ever extracted from the world's ponds."

"Over here, Skotos, it's time I show you something." I couldn't wait to see the look on my boy's face. "Welcome to deception's treasure chest! This is what hope-deferred has allowed us to steal: dreams! We've taken the multitude of unique dreams from the many and traded them one big, manufactured, boxed dream in return. Though we couldn't literally kill the dreams of their hearts, when their hope was deferred and their hearts grew cold, they freely gave away these living organisms of hope. We can't use them of course, but neither can they as long as they remain blind to their loss. We've acquired most of these dreams on the cheap, we simply wait for the opportune moment in time, when hope runs dry and nearly any offer we present conjures up enough temporary satisfaction they truly have no clue what they're giving up. And so grows our treasure."

I don't think Skotos could believe it, I had been holding this secret place for a time like now, when he was fully ready to appreciate the dormant hope we possessed. I marveled watching him marvel.

"Father, what's this?" Skotos asked while picking up a colorful kite of simple appearance. "I don't doubt what you're saying, it's just hard to see treasure in something as simple as a kite."

"Oh, but Son, that kite you hold was once the favorite childhood toy of one of the most powerful women in America. When she was a child her heart flew as high as the kite did running freely through the park. When the kite went up, so did her spirit. When we took the kite and labeled it the frivolous childhood toy they've since referred to it as, well, she also gave us much of what was attached to the kite, the first and most foundational parts of her freedom to dream. Skotos, you see, this woman didn't just let go of the kite, she let go of the park it led her to, the wild and exhilarating running down the hills, the wind that could carry her imagination elsewhere, the joy of the skies, and especially the impossible belief that was so natural to her once powerfully childlike nature. This kite is a prime example of all these treasures that each represent the fertile ground which could be the foundation of every heart, where new dreams would certainly spring to life."

"Wow, Dad, I had no idea! But why did you wait until now to bring me?"

"This is our greatest secret, most of the wolves don't

even know it exists, or else, they might scheme for these dreams for themselves. Look at this one, Son. Can you imagine if someone rediscovered this dream in their lives? It's the opposite of the societal culture we have created." I watched my son squint his eyes tightly trying to see correctly. The treasure I held bore resemblance to an old figurine, what most now refer to as action figures. Do you know, Skotos, who this is?"

"No, Dad, I have no clue. Who?"

"This is Johnny Appleseed, an early pioneer and frontiersman who knew the power of a seed. Anyone who knows hope knows that all you need is a seed. A seed culture of hope would be the end of our kind, not at first, but slowly over time. Part of the lies of self we feed are to create the insatiable need for instant gratification—the very opposite of a seed! Plant enough seeds in the most barren of wilderness, and it's not long before its barrenness is overtaken, creating a fruitful paradise. The little boy who used to play with this toy loved to imagine himself out on the frontier, traveling with this Appleseed fellow while he planted hope of one tree after another. This boy began to dream of being a pioneer himself, a pioneer of hope lived out by who knows what, perhaps even planting seeds of hope in various people's lives, giving generously and the like. This little figurine taught the boy to dream big dreams. But you know what that little boy does now, now that this treasure is in our hands? He's the biggest suburban home developer in the nation, shredding tree filled forests all over the country without conscience, trading one lush green for another. He went the opposite way of where the child in him was headed. When we convinced him to leave this treasure for one of ours, you know, the gold, silver and green kind, he caused us no threat anymore. I have his dream while he's livin' mine!"

"Skotos, everything in here represents a part of them that we labeled for them as childish and insignificant as they grew. It wasn't about the items as much as the portal of imaginative belief and wonder these items can open up. We have a room full of what once brought people joy, what inspired them to use their imagination, to believe in more than self; the trinkets and toys that helped them see life differently through clear lenses, and we've sold them overpriced sunglasses instead. They can look glamorous all they want as long as they don't see, nor recover, the seeds of their former dreams. From those seeds, one's imagination can cause such dreams to grow far, and fast. And such a world would then be out of our reach. That is why this secret of a treasure is so vital to our livelihood, and our growth. Few have any idea where to look, and of those that do, well, most of them are too afraid of wolves." I wrapped it up with a big deceivingly happy smile at my boy.

"Skotos, I want you to keep it that way."

Chapter 6:
The Third Dream:
Seeing in the Dark

"What lies behind us and what lies ahead of us are tiny matters compared to what lives in us."

- Henry David Thoreau

I opened my eyes to find I was in mid-air, soaring high above rugged but beautiful terrain. It had to be the most fun beginning to a dream I had ever experienced. It didn't look like we were in my neighboring Rocky Mountains anymore, this was an entirely different kind of mountainous landscape—*but beautiful!*

I was in the grasp of what had to be the largest, most powerful talons on the planet, yet there wasn't an ounce of discomfort. They weren't sharp in the way that I might have feared. And how he was managing to hold me, well, that thought was far less meaningful than the many other questions I already had listed in my heart. Although, something was telling me that *my* questions weren't really going to be setting the agenda. I was…we were flying, but I could hardly get out of my own head enough to enjoy what for most people would have been quite a dream. Isn't it funny how that works? We can dream of something like flying and the rush it might bring, but often when we get in the middle of a true adventure we start nervously searching for somewhere to put our feet, or at least somewhere grounded and secure for our thoughts.

Recognizing this, I decided to will myself out of my immediate reaction because I wanted to take all this in with fresh perspective. Who knows how many dreams I had already missed in life, having been in the middle of them but unable to receive something new they were offering. That's something I was continuing to learn through all this. I, like many others I suppose, had been crying out for something new to give me hope. But often, the problem with something new is—it usually requires something new. I was desperate for a new answer in my life, but didn't always like to receive the answer when it came in an unknown or surprising package. The irony.

I looked down again, and then glanced back up at Founder. It seemed he was locked in on a destination. I asked several times where we were going, but he wouldn't say. The surprise was quickly becoming a big part of the adventure. I looked back down and decided I would see for myself. What a world! The terrain was a gift in itself. I couldn't recognize any of it though. Wherever we were was brand new to me.

I felt my right shoulder dip down, and my left side rose suddenly. We were obviously turning, but the learning curve in these dreams had me processing a little slower it seemed. Founder swooped us to the east and we started to slowly descend but our speed stayed virtually the same. Founder was so smooth in flight, I could barely tell the difference between when he flapped his wings versus simply gliding. The feeling was almost unspeakable. But there it was, just below us, what I assumed was our destination. Now I knew where we were, and could confirm I had never been here before either. Mt. Rushmore!

What a sight, and from this perspective flying in over it added that much more amazement. The rugged rocks painted such a beautiful picture and within just a moment I already had a new appreciation for these leaders, pioneers who paved the way to all we were—*or could*—be living. I never thought I would enjoy Mt. Rushmore this much. Always thought it was a basic tourist attraction, almost familiar from all the pictures. However, none of those postcards had done *this* any justice.

We curved right down around the edge, just past the enormous bust of Abraham Lincoln himself. Wow! Speechless. "Brace yourself," Founder stated quickly. We soared back up over the head of Mr. Jefferson and landed abruptly just above and behind the right side of the head of President Roosevelt. Wow! What a ride!

"Did you have fun?" Founder asked.

"Fun, I barely had time for fun. But, I tried to make some time anyway. I'm learning that sometimes enjoying what is right in front of you, no matter how much you want it, it can still be a real discipline." Founder laughed. He seemed a little more easygoing than previously, a tone that seemed to come from our location.

"This is one of my most cherished places."

"Mt. Rushmore?" I asked.

"Mt. Rushmore is beautiful, and is an incredible portrayal of why we are here, but my special spot is actually down inside."

"Inside?" I asked with a little hesitation, and a lot of surprise. "What's inside?"

"I'll show you," he said, though he was already eagerly moving towards something or somewhere before he even spoke.

I followed him a few steps down and around several rocks where Founder was now perched on the ground and looking deeply into a hole. "It's a cave," Founder announced fondly.

"A cave? No thank you. I'm not really interest…."

"Oh, come on, Will. Come closer and have a look for yourself. You want to endeavor into new perspectives, right?"

"Well, yes, but…"

"Come on then, just right here."

Founder pointed to a spot directly in front of him, a hole in the ground hardly suited for an eagle, and now seemingly pointing back at me. I took a couple more steps until I could see down inside. I didn't see any evidence of a cave, just a very dark, open space surrounded by weeds that looked like a home for the world's largest groundhog. What could Founder possibly love inside this place? How does an eagle even fly down such a forsaken place, I murmured in my mind.

"Like this!" Founder yelled with a laugh, extending his wings with a push to my back, thrusting me down what might as well have been a monumental waterslide. The fall didn't last for long, landing right on my backside onto what felt like a pile of pillowy pine needles.

"How do you like my nest?" Founder yelled down

with far more joy than I currently had at the moment. But I had to admit, it was fun experiencing this side of Founder, even if it was at my expense. "You're lucky I like my nests on the comfy side, Will, good for the wings that way."

"Nest, huh? Okay, I'm down here already. What about you?" I couldn't even finish my question before he was tapping me on my shoulder with his wing. "Gosh, you scared me," I blurted out. It was a deep black I'd never seen before, and my eyes seemed kind of worthless, seeing nothing. I couldn't see Founder, his nest, how or when he came down or even myself.

"This is the greatest training ground and the origin of true vision," Founder stated, back to the normal tone he holds when on a mission.

"But I can't see anything at all."

"Precisely," he responded. "If you can't see in the dark, you can't see any differently than anyone else. Vision doesn't come from your circumstances, so it should not be limited by your circumstances either. Until you learn to see in the dark, you can't really see at all."

Now it seemed like he was talking in puzzles, but I was already becoming such a different person in his company, I knew I had to buckle down my own thoughts and keep learning, even if it did just feel like I was humoring him at first. If I truly wanted to live the dreams and desires that Founder said were already hidden within me, then they'd likely come by a path that was new to me as well.

"Your eyes always play tricks on you, fed by many different things. But your vision and heart perspective never need to change. It is up to each individual to choose which one they will live by. Sheep live by what they can see, and wolves steal their vision, much like you didn't realize at our first meeting in the zoo. If you live for what you can see, you will never have a chance at living the dream. It's not until you begin walking on the bridge that is vision that you can truly cross over into a better life, by heart standards that is. Sheep standards have to go, or you will keep yourself double minded between your sight and your vision."

"Only you can choose which you will live by, and you cannot try to have both. Choose sight, and you will lose vision at the expense of the pride of culture. Choose vision, and before you know it you will actually have an eye for all the life vision lives to give back. This cave, though dark, is the heart of where true hope begins. It is in the dark that the greatest truths can be revealed to you, a breeding ground for stark contrasts to reveal themselves, where you can discover all that sight could never give you."

I stumbled forward, trying to prove his words with my steps.

"I appreciate your eagerness, Will, but it is not that simple. Don't hurt yourself with lack of patience just to throw out this new path altogether. Patience is essential for real vision to come to life."

I could already feel a bruise just under my knee, but still, I couldn't even see Founder here.

"But you know my voice," Founder interrupted.

"Yeah, you're right."

"Step back where you started, back to the middle of the nest you fell into."

"Ohh-kaayy," I answered with pause, constantly finding myself in the middle of that reluctant desire that I had to keep fighting myself over.

"Stand up straight," he said plainly. And just then he gave me a firm nudge in the opposite direction I had begun, pushing me out of the nest like an eagle might its own. It felt vicious, not in severity but intention, like an attack even, but I landed on my feet. And when I looked up I could see one small gleam of light, like a single star in the night was staring back at me. It was distant but inviting, like it was waiting for me to join it on the miniature path of light it sprayed at my feet. I couldn't see any such light before, not even a morsel from where I first stood. But now, there it was.

"Just trust me," said Founder.

"I wish it were that easy," I responded sheepishly.

"It is that easy," Founder responded. I always forget just how deep that bird can hear. I chuckled, and so did he. "Walk towards the light. And think about this for a second. If it wasn't so dark, would you even be able to find that particular light?"

Wow, what a question. I had never thought of it in such a way, such a highlighted path really would be drowned out in most normal environments, perhaps never found. One point for Founder I thought to myself. My heart suddenly felt primed for adventure, less afraid, hands on and revving my own engine for what might come next. Founder started up again.

"Too often we allow darkness to intimidate us, rather than sharpen us while taking our blade to its grip. It is far too common when surrounded by the dark to blend in, even when that was the opposite of one's original desire and intent. Why? It's because it feels safe. It feels more secure to blend into the darkness than to venture through the unknown. It takes courage to live a true dream, and real dreams aren't lived without conquering dark paths. The true reality is that darkness should point you in the direction of the light. The darkness doesn't have to be an enemy, when it can be an usher, helping to highlight to you your awaiting seat of destiny. If this were a cave of light, how easy would it be to miss your true calling? Darkness allows the calling of your purpose to call more loudly to you. It is part of becoming who you are, as you will live out much of what you conquer. Such victories will give you vision for what is increasingly possible."

If there were ever words to take away my fear for the dark, though a weighty subject, these were the ones. The wisdom that came from this new friend continued to shame much of what I knew, had been taught, or what I usually lived by. He shared an upside-down perspective making me forget which direction the roof was. And maybe, I suppose I was learning that there really didn't have to be a roof at all.

"Keep walking towards that small glimmer of light. The darkness around you may appear large, while the light still seems to keep a secret agent like profile, for now. But when you narrow the focus of your vision, the darkness shrinks and the light grows stronger, strong enough to compel you forward far beyond the reach of the dark. Each one grows at the power of your choosing, being enlarged by where you offer your attention. One gleam of light, a tiny reflection, is all you need when you see it through hope's lens. It will become an everlasting path that shows you a different way to live your dreams, no matter the circumstance. The power is in the choice of where you place your vision. Your choices resurrect vision from the tomb it appeared to be buried within, and you get to live it out to life. Let me know, would you Will, when we are near the light at the end of the tunnel?"

It appeared to me we were almost there, about to break out of this dark enclosure, like the gasp of air I had dreamt of finding. And even though I was learning, I still wanted out—badly. Based on Founder's question, I felt it was a confirmation that we were indeed getting close. I took about fifteen more long strides, each time cautiously planting one foot before the other. My arm reached out before me like it didn't even need my permission, exploring further than I could will it to search, or so it seemed.

"Okay, we're here," I stated with confidence.

"Here? Where's here?" Founder quipped back.

"We're at the light; so where is the door out?"

"Out? Why would you want to go out? The goal is not to leave the darkness, but to have such a vision that brings light in here. There's too much darkness in the world always to try and find an escape. You'll always be running that way. What appear to be troubles can be an invitation for you to rise with new light. Too many people want to leave their problems, if not just ask for answers. True vision for life offers answers that have long been buried in the dark; answers that make the wolves of culture no longer want to come out at night. When your view of light is changed, so too will the darkness of this room be kicked out on its keester."

Can't say I had ever heard that word spoken much, but then again, I hadn't had conversations with many eagles either, he obviously shared a vocabulary with my

Grandpa. I felt like I was trying to solve a riddle, but I couldn't tell if that riddle was in the cave, or in my own mind. "When my view of light is changed?" I repeated Founder's question to myself, sometimes out loud, other times within my thoughts. "Light?" I started to ponder his query more deeply, perhaps making it more complex than necessary. I tried unpacking the concept of darkness as well, but it wasn't getting me anywhere. Founder stood there patiently, or so I thought. That's what his silence told me anyway.

"So many people think about or look for the light at the end of the tunnel," Founder intervened. "What would you think about letting light into the tunnel?"

"Huh?"

It almost made too much sense. Believing anything else almost seemed counter intuitive. "Why wasn't I taught to think that way?"

"In your culture, many have an expectation of a falsely projected dream that is lived towards them. But in created culture, naturally, there is a dream in you that wants to live out to the world. Many are so busy expecting such a dream to come to them they can't live out the bigger possibilities that are well within reach. They've lost their vision, and without vision, the people will perish. When you begin to step past your old limits you will unlock a new you that breathes the very hope that you long for. It's already breathing inside you. But it takes a first step, and that step is often the hardest. It is usually counter-cultural by nature, and many times it is actually the most obvious. Will, reach out your hand towards the light."

Immediately I listened and did as Founder suggested. But as I reached, I thought of something. Or perhaps simply what Founder had been saying found me. Instead of trying to find a door, or push out into the light I put two fingers as far as I could into the light, gripped what I could and pulled back towards me, into the tunnel as he had so uniquely encouraged. A flood of hundreds of small rocks began to tumble and the light caved in on us one pebble at a time. It wasn't a door, but a window, and though I couldn't get out of it the window shone enough light to transform the room, and for me to see it for what it really was, a cave of mirrors.

They weren't actual mirrors, but they might as well have been. And the first thing I saw reflected was the image of Founder rolling around the ground in utter laughter.

"Yes, yes, you've completed your grand experiment. Did you stack each of those pebbles yourself?" I asked him sarcastically.

"As a matter of fact I…"

"Alright, I got it, no need to answer that one," I stopped him, shaking my head.

All around us were translucent rocks, crystal like, and they all seemed to be dancing with the light in a reflective tone. Almost made me want to join in—*almost*. They truly made it look like we were surrounded by hundreds of mirrors, and each one had a uniqueness of its own.

"Other than in darkness, this is where vision is most learned," Founder continued. "You may call it the Cave of Mirrors, I call it the Cave of Identity. Similar to the question I first asked you about yourself up on the Ridge of Hope, it is that same question you are helped to answer here. 'What do you see?' If you do not learn to see yourself correctly, you will not be able to see anyone, or anything else correctly either. You will stay a sheep until you learn to see yourself differently than the up and down images you have grown up with. You must learn here *how* to see yourself. You are not a reflection of other people's thoughts or opinions, or your own accomplishments or lack thereof. You are not a reflection of results, but of the heart and its perspectives. You can only see yourself correctly through light as it pierces the darkness. The same darkness the wolves thrive within."

"When you change the way you see yourself, you give yourself permission to change the world around you. When you cease from seeing the sheep the wolves want you to see when looking in that mirror, you render the wolves toothless and can start to sink your own teeth into new, truly potential filled dreams."

I looked up to study my reflection, and was

encouraged by the mirrors. They were a leg to stand on in answering the question of what I saw, much more so than on the mountaintop. Though I will never forget the incredible insights Founder injected into me there either, and perhaps a primary reason why I even had the ability to look into such a mirror. I could very nearly see the shadows of what I *was* warring against, whom the light was trying to prove me to be.

No matter how hard I strained to see myself, all I could think of was a sheep. Even when I desperately sought more, it was like my own mind was afraid of letting me out of its more comfortable routines, constantly pulling the wool over my own eyes and fixated on the past. What I needed was a vision that could pierce through the thickest of wool and overcome the wolves I had allowed to den up in my mind for far too long.

That's when it hit me, what Founder had so wisely forecasted regarding the light. I was still limiting myself by staring at what was the result of the light, but really, he said I needed to look with and *through the light*! I turned my position about ninety degrees, and could at the same time see a flicker of hope in Founder's eye, just enough to light a fire under any self doubt I had left. I looked up to the mirror like creation now before me; what it portrayed was unlike any reflection I had seen in my life. The reflection itself was three-dimensional, like a hologram. The way the light reflected with the natural building blocks all around me revealed parts of me that can't usually be seen in a typical mirror, underlying treasures somewhere inside me which left me without words to describe, there was so much more I had yet to put to use. I had been blind to them all along.

"The unique reflection you're seeing means you are starting to see yourself from a higher perspective. You come from a culture where so much is lived out as black and white, where worth is result-oriented, and value comes from one extreme or another—too often missing out on the hidden answers in between. Not until the 'be' and the 'who' overtake the 'what' and the 'do' will a culture such as yours know true value—in yourselves or one another. You're seeing parts of yourself that you've been taught to ignore, or compelled not to look at. You have probably often heard that still small voice inside you trying to shepherd your sheep like nature in the right direction, but that voice is difficult to hear when competing against a culture of howling wolves you have esteemed more highly, who are to say the least desperate to blind you from hidden truth. When you learn to see yourself in this updated fashion you will unlock more doors of hope than you will ever have time to explore. The world truly is full of unveiled hope, but you have been taught to live life through veils that render you blind to the truth the wolves have under their feet. Allow the veils to be torn and you will have enough dreams to lend to others until they rediscover their own. Hope will then prevail endlessly. Find your identity, silence the wolves."

Now, when I stared into that mirror I saw something I never knew I had, or perhaps simply misjudged its position in my life, a horizon, though I couldn't yet tell what was upon it. Regardless of that, a horizon was the very definition of hope, even if I didn't know yet what flavor that hope would bring. From everything I was learning, I think a large part of that flavor was up to me. Did I want Cookies 'n' Cream, or Rocky Road? I was good with either one, or, if it truly was my horizon, how about a scoop of each?

Staring into the mirror this time didn't seem so much about what my eyes laid hold of, but perhaps what I didn't see anymore. I didn't see my old life. I didn't see all my regrets bogging down my skies with their dirty exhaust, or the horrendous fumes that usually accompanied such memories. I didn't see through a lens of hopelessness, fear, or want. I didn't see any sheep at all. All I saw was a horizon of possibility. The same horizon that seemed to be hidden by the smog of our culture was actually very bright still in me, the two had surely warred against one another all these years. I had allowed the outside to dictate what was in me, instead of the other way around. The light in my reflection burned away all the fears of what I might see, or perhaps now they were just the fears I once had. The light consumed my reflection to such a level that it was like the sunrise I often saw at home, the ones I look into that blur my actual ability to see. That's what my life looked like in this mirror, from this perspective. The old had blurred unrecognizable, and the new was grossly possible. In fact, all I could see was light—*hope's own glare!* It was the first canvas I'd seen in years that hadn't been soiled with fear, and this one actually invited *me* to paint. What was on the horizon was clearly awaiting my brush, of which I didn't have any at home, but my heart was starting to discover quite a few new techniques from within. There was much to be learned, but my new picture wouldn't be dictated by anyone else, and that was a freedom I was finally learning to receive.

Founder spoke up and joined me in my thoughts.

"When you see with the light, even in the darkness, it's amazing how it renews your perspective. The light is a vision of you that has yet to be defined. As you become less defined by the culture of sight that you grew up in, the dark parts of the world will have far less affect on you. The light is a culture of vision. It possesses the secrets, and the adventures, that you and so many others are looking for, where true freedom comes willingly alive! It is the pursuit on the way to happiness. Light removes the condemnation of old, and puts the horizon in your very own hands and choices. Now that you see yourself correctly in the light, despite the darkness, you will begin to have dreams that can be seen. Your identity, or the potential for such, is a powerful, life-giving sunrise on a dawn where the howls at the moon begin to fade away. The joy isn't just in the fact that darkness is ending, but that the day is only beginning, and a new horizon there to be seized."

****

I remember sitting straight up in bed like I was still sleeping in the cave, alert for predators. I was out of breath and felt like I had aged five years based on all Founder poured in. My world seemed bigger. No longer did it seem like it was closing in on me, but it was now a world where light and opportunity were seemingly waiting to be unearthed. But, I could literally smell the odor of my daily routines set out before me, like a boiled egg cooked too many days in advance. I could taste something different, but the world wanted to give me the old. I couldn't control that part—that which the world gave me—but I could change how I saw myself, and start new from there. And for that day, that was enough of a change to help me smile even through finishing that old boiled egg at breakfast.

Chapter 7:
Culture Wars

"Every man must decide whether he will walk in the light of creative altruism or in the darkness of destructive selfishness." - Dr. Martin Luther King Jr.

Unfortunately, my struggle that next day did not stop at the breakfast table. Looking back, the day after visiting Mt. Rushmore and the Cave of Identity was one of the most difficult days I can remember, even amid a long line of duds. It left me with a question I battled often for quite some time thereafter: What do you do when two cultures collide? There was the culture I was learning, one of vision and hope, a culture that saw me completely differently than I had ever seen myself. And then there was the culture I had grown up with, the one I had come to expect and the very same that others definitely expected of me, this culture that had me uncomfortably comfortable, with shallow expectations of myself. It was a culture where I counted sheep at night, desperate to fall asleep to escape the challenges of the day that were trying to drag on in my mind. This question and its battle within me became what I started to refer to as the culture wars, battles within me for with which eyes I would see.

My little brother, David, was home sick that day. And though he could be a challenge for me, it was the related tension of the house that really posed a threat. He had special classes at his school for much of what he battled, care that Mom didn't seem to have the patience for anymore, and that which Dad wasn't around to really even know about. So, Mom was home with him and I was somewhere in the middle, once again caught in between. She kept me home that day too. I wasn't sick, in fact I felt like I was starting to get better for the very first time! No, mom wanted my help. Well, I wasn't much help, so perhaps she just wanted my company, even if she couldn't say so. Mom was loving and kind, but had become distant. Not just distant from us, I felt like she was even distant from herself if that makes any sense, like she had trouble exhaling. I think I understood more than she knew, sensing she probably felt a lot of the same things I did; fear, lack of hope, like the walls of the house were sneaking in closer, inch by inch, every day. But she's "the Mom", and probably doesn't feel free to give herself room for weakness. I wished she would. There's something liberating about admitting weakness, it seems some supernatural strength is suddenly given the room it needs to make it's way back in, like hot air filling the balloon that's fallen flat, waiting and wanting to make its way back up into the skies again, even lifting others up in the process. I think I took on a lot of what I felt from Mom, bearing her burdens while she feared not being able to bear mine. But things were changing for me, if not yet on the outside.

On the inside I wanted to shout from the rooftops, singing out all that was happening inside me like a new life song. On the outside, I was afraid. Mom was definitely on edge that day. She had been feeling much better, but still didn't have her strength back. And she was really ticked at Dad, probably bitter over the things she was doing that he wasn't. David was bedridden with the flu, but that didn't totally stop his insides from wanting to go warp speed. And me, though I was overflowing with excitement about the adventures and lessons of my nights, I didn't exactly know how to handle it yet. I didn't have the patience I should have after such a high in my own life. Others had old expectations of me, and I had new ones of them, even if I could feel what they were going through deep down, it didn't change the atmosphere of hot air without the balloon on the outside. I didn't want to be held in that place anymore, but truly, it probably wasn't fair of me to expect anything different yet either. I mean, I was only beginning to dream so differently, and as far as I could tell they hadn't been privy to such dreams.

More than anything, the culture of this life was almost exaggerated to me, *even more than before*, which was pretty hard to believe. That was a good thing, and at the same time, not so good. Every smell, routine or expectation was heightened, and would make me more upset. The curtained light seemed dimmer, the skylight and the sun couldn't seem to line up, and the pungent smell of routine made me feel like I was the one with the flu. That was not a good mix with all the other strife in the home already, just made me add to it. Since then, I've learned to handle it much better, and see a little deeper with how to live it out. But at that point, the culture wars in me were raging. I was tired of the everyday routines that we called "normal." I didn't want a fast-food life anymore, but even beyond my own heightened senses I started to realize that it was literally everywhere I went, and mostly spoon-fed like processed peas, only not so green if you know what I mean. It seemed the "dream" we were living was actually a box, with the real dream running free on the outside faster than anyone could keep up, like it was fleeing the seen. I felt duped into a false happiness in such a boxed life. I wanted the pursuit of such happiness I could only find outside that box, maybe back in the air like that terrifying approach to Mt. Rushmore.

I think we find the box comfortable, and a nice

measuring stick of who can rise to the top. But in reality, the top of the box is still just the top of the box. Once you get up there, it's only a matter of time before you hit the ground again and have to find another ladder up, often at the expense of others, leaving a footprint on someone else's face and covering their eyes for our own survival. I dreamt of blowing the lid off that box, for my sake and for whoever else might want to fly a little. I know I did. Founder had only strengthened that dream, a dream I probably didn't even know I had until such midnight adventures began. Founder lit a match to something in me that just wasn't the same, and my perspective of most things was suddenly in even more disarray, confused how to walk between the two.

I just tried to survive that day, which truly, was the opposite of the way I was being taught to live. It was more difficult than I thought to teach an old sheep new perspective. Something I was sure Founder would have something to say about that night, or at least I hoped he would. I remember it vividly; I couldn't wait to get to sleep! I was running away from the day and into the night where I assumed true dreams were awaiting me. And true dreams probably were awaiting me, perhaps just not in the way I knew quite yet.

I finished dinner quickly that night. I still had homework from the day before and I had wanted to finish up so as to drift off early into the life I was yearning for. But even once I got under those newly trusted covers, I still couldn't sleep. I had the residual frustration from my day lingering overhead, and no peace to counter it. All night I tossed and turned and wrestled with myself, afraid I was back to my old battles against the nights instead of the new version cheering me on. Nothing! I was exhausted, probably from my efforts more than it was from not sleeping. Though I'm sure that didn't help either. What was the deal? Had Founder abandoned me now? I knew I wasn't ready yet. I thought our journey was just beginning. Had I lost the dreams I was just starting to learn?

The clock hit 6:45am and I still hadn't slept much. I certainly hadn't dreamt, at least not that I knew of. That day I rolled out of bed, stood over the sink to brush my teeth and felt sick. I wasn't literally or physically sick, but felt like I had just been through a bitter war with myself, and the wolves of my house. They were probably in all actuality my own wolves that I allowed in, but I often found myself attributing them to others.

I stumbled down the stairs with the last bit of joy drooping off my face and sat down for yep, you guessed it, another old boiled egg. I had a really bad attitude that morning. And Mom could see it, or she could see something. I don't know if she was trying to compensate for her usual distance and have pity on me, or if she really thought I had David's bug, but she immediately told me to get upstairs and into bed, strictly warning me against getting her or anyone else sick. I let her believe what she wanted to. I didn't have much in my tank to make it through school anyway. I wasn't in the mood to get in bed though. Even though I hadn't slept, I remember being upset at the battle my bed had been the stage for all night. I sat down on the floor, leaned up against the bed and got lost somewhere in my iPod. That didn't last long though. I must have passed out pretty quickly that day, because I didn't wake up until dinner, and I woke up having slept all day on the floor. But thankfully, comfort no longer dictated my dreams.

Chapter 8:
The Fourth Dream:
Dr. King & Me

"History will have to record that the greatest tragedy of this period of social transition was not the strident clamor of the bad people, but the appalling silence of the good people." - Dr. Martin Luther King Jr.

The sun was beating down on the bright white of the sidewalk under my feet. In fact, I was literally surrounded by cement. Its glaring reflection was almost inescapable, a blank canvas almost too white as I waited to see what it would reveal. These surroundings were new to me, but easy to recognize. Carefully and ceremoniously sculpted monuments stood everywhere I looked. I was in Washington D.C. and Founder was perched properly upright on the tall, strong memorial before me. With his head tilted down and cocked to the side, he looked at me with striking purpose—almost nodding in agreement as I recognized just where he was perched, on the broad shoulders of one Martin Luther King Jr. It wasn't the real Dr. King, of course, but the newly erected monument that memorialized him. Though I didn't know all the details to appreciate from his life, I respected this legend I'd heard spoken of so favorably, and I certainly appreciated the extra time off school each year in his honor.

"I was there, you know," Founder said with as much pride as I'd ever heard bellow out from underneath his words, perching even a little bit taller now. "The day Dr. King stood face to face with a previously all too accepted lie of the wolves, I circled above the crowd that was gathered around him, but low enough for earshot. I listened to him denounce lies and declare freedom's dream—every last word of it! I've seen and experienced a lot of things, but I don't know if there's ever been anyone among your culture of man that has stirred my spirit or lifted my wings like Martin Luther King Jr."

I listened in awe, and almost disbelief, trying to picture what it must have been like, what Founder must have felt while circling overhead. It was years before I was born, but Founder spoke of it like it was yesterday. It was more a monumental day to him than this giant statue could even begin to commemorate. I loved hearing him talk with such passion, bursting through his feathers. It was an incredible compliment to the wisdom he already overflowed so naturally.

"Dr. King represented the very foundation of who I am and why I exist." Founder stated plainly. "He made the freedom of my wings bigger, broader, and brighter. He carried a presence about him—and especially on that day—that represents my hope for this nation and your culture in such a variety of ways. If there was ever a man I personally witnessed live inside out, it was Dr. King. I want to see his dream multiplied through many more and see every injustice be overcome."

"The atmosphere of that day," Founder continued, "was only heightened under the shadow of Lincoln's memorial where we stood. I could feel anticipation in the air, and watched as each listener hung on his every word, as if the wings of such a national culture hung in the balance; mine included. I listened like I had never listened before, not simply to his words but also to the spirit of freedom that broke out and continued to rise in each heart present or listening, viral freedom. Each heart was inspired and empowered to partake of a new dream at a time when so much of the nation was either grasping for life, or at one another. Hope breathed that day. Millions were infected with hope, and millions more thereafter. Dr. King put a seed in the heart of a nation, a seed that would help a hurting people to dream, again. Dr. King is a beautiful picture of why you can meet me here in your dreams today."

Founder continued speaking, and as much as I loved hearing the perspective that flowed through him so naturally, part of me wished I too could be hearing Dr. King's own voice.

"You can," Founder interrupted my daydreaming, as he frequently had. "In fact, that is why we are here. I believe Dr. King's voice, and even more—*his dream*—can come alive inside *you.*"

"Really?" I stood there a little wide-eyed. While thrilled with the idea, I still was more than a little perplexed as to what exactly that might mean. But such were the ways of my feathered companion; there was always a deeper, hidden truth he was helping me to see. It was the literal version of what Founder said that excited me, and that didn't seem too possible, obviously.

"Oh, but it is, Will!" Founder responded swiftly, once again with some trick up his sleeve to be sure.

"There are voices of hope inside you that are brimming and ready to burst into your life, as well as the lives of others who wait for the dream in you to become a life-changing reality. You just haven't allowed yourself— nor been taught—to be privy to them, *yet!* You may have many outlets to learn about Dr. King, but what if the world could learn his same nature through you? What if Dr. King's voice, or better yet the very voice of truth and freedom inside you would be allowed to escape from its dormant fire in your belly the same way Martin Luther King Jr. quieted his own fears long enough to let such a voice emerge? You think it was easy for him? Do you actually believe such courageous thinking and living came without a fight inside and out? That's not how it works, Will. In a culture among wolves, a dream must be fought for before hope's reality ever seems possible, and that battle starts deep inside you. Can you imagine the many hidden, lonely, painful moments Dr. King must have endured to see such a battle, such a dream become a seen reality? Dr. King lived his dream inside through the clenched jaws of many wolves before he publicly rendered their lies a thing of the past, and led many sheep to greener pastures. The battle is private before it is public. You have seen or heard but a percentage point of Dr. King's life, think about how he must have battled and lived, and persevered through all those unseen moments none of us have ever heard about. And you wonder why his voice is so strong, because first he conquered the dissenting voices within himself, so that the real Martin could be free, and heard."

The idea in itself seemed radical. I saw nothing in my life that compared to that of Dr. King, and even if I did, I wasn't sure I had the courage to live it out. I looked up to the standing monument where Dr. King stared resolutely over my head. In fact, the whole idea felt over my head.

But then again I suppose that was why we were here—to raise my game a little, but this seemed like more than a little. I have to hand it to Founder; he had picked quite the measuring stick. I'd have to rise significantly higher to even look this monument of a man in the eyes. However, in thinking about it, such a rising journey sounded pretty on par with where Founder had been leading me all along. I understood what he was implying. It wasn't just Dr. King's superb message I was to carry, it was his spirit that lived such a powerful dream and which empowered so many into their own previously unfathomed possibilities.

"Will, I want you to read this. This here is the vision statement of the memorial."

I began reading and finished it quickly. But I felt blank, as if I hadn't caught a thing. I read it again and still couldn't get it to stick, it was one of those times when you can read something over and over without ever actually *reading it,* let alone understanding what is being offered.

"Relax, Will. You're putting too much pressure on yourself, stop trying so hard. Listen to the words. Let the words wash over you and try to see the world through them, allow them to be like new glasses that change your perception of what's possible. See the words not just for their definition, but according to what they have the potential to mean to you, *and through you.*"

I started reading again and just a sentence or two in found myself uncharacteristically reading aloud; something had obviously struck a cord. Out of the corner of my eye I saw Founder reading with me, a much needed encouragement. *"…His vision of America is captured in his message of hope and possibility,"* I read again. Those two words—*hope and possibility*—were in themselves music to my ears. Possibility in my life had been dim for so long before these journeys began with Founder, but I couldn't stop there. *"Anchored in dignity, sensitivity, and mutual respect; a message that challenges each of us to recognize that America's true strength lies in its diversity of talents."* I couldn't be sure if I was processing the words, or if they were processing me. I was chewing on them, like a cow and its cud, berating them over and again long after they lost their taste but still hoping to extract some more 'nutritional' value. *"Recognize that America's true strength lies in its diversity of talents,"* I repeated once more. Something struck me, but I couldn't piece it all together, let alone figure out which piece I held.

"Have I ever told you about my grandmother, Will? She told the greatest stories and had some of the very best advice. It was my grandfather who held such a distinguished role on behalf of this nation, yet she was the flag of strength behind him that epitomized such a life lived out."

"She often told me a story of a quilt made by a very important woman in this nation as she taught me how to build a proper nest. Now, she knew that I was in line for our family's bronzed perch, but she always assured me that nothing replaced a good nest. She made me promise that no family of mine would ever rest in a subpar nest, just as she watched the quilt of that one particular woman always provide the seamless warmth it intended."

"She talked about the power of a quilt and the diverse place each square of fabric might originate from. That's the beauty of a quilt, you know? They're not beautiful for being made up all from the same most luxurious fabrics and design. It's the diversity in a quilt that brings that extra measure of warmth, and even more, that extra kind of special. It's the contrast that makes the compliment, each piece crying out for the others. The same is true of a good nest. The best nests are made from such a variety of ingredients, each one standing out to hold its own. We pull twigs and branches from so many diverse trees and locations, and even those are still complimented by grasses, cornstalks, mosses and many other unique but essential parts. The diversity of which makes it that much stronger, at least when each are living up to its own special purpose and part. Our dreams are much the same way with their own contrasting compliments and their ability to change the world. There are too many essentially unique pieces for anything to be so broadly called 'the dream.' My dream is everyone living the one they have been created for. And Dr. King already reset the stage."

"Will, how do you help people achieve a widespread diversity of talents such as this? You give them permission to dream. Dr. King is not just about the dream that he held and inspired. *He is about so much more!* Martin Luther King Jr. is an inspiration of the true American dream that has become so lost today. He is a model of what many dreams *could* still become. The fact that he had a dream was a dream in itself. To have such a bold, courageous vision is what leads you into your own diverse talent in the world. So many people would love to have a statue or monument of their life by the time they are gone, but few are willing to dream it out loud the way Dr. King did. And to be honest, the monument hardly matters, the dream does. We celebrate Dr. King's message, as we most definitely should. But what if we celebrated his example in a broad diversity of ways, in regards to an array of different subjects and injustices? America's strength would rise again. People would be less busy measuring up to one another and the false dream it's become to be much more focused on living the unique dream that is alive in them. The fact that Dr. King had a dream was monumental. The fact that he lived it out the way he did was beyond compare. The conviction of his message changed the world. How might the world be changed if you lived out the conviction of the dream that's alive in you? I already see it, Will. But, do you? Will you even allow yourself to see what's already there?"

My heart raced with Founder's message. To say it was convincing is a grave understatement, convicting too.

Had I been waiting all this time for a dream to come to me rather than recognizing the dream that was waiting for me? And he was right, he was helping the spirit of MLK Jr. come alive in me. I heard a voice in me that wanted out. It often tried to pound down my all too frequent self-imposed limits, heart rumbling up into my throat while the fear somewhere in my head tried to spew out such fire.

"Will, what would Dr. King say to you? What is the injustice burning in your heart he would speak to? What is the change you want to see in the world? What is your dream? The current American dream has become a race to conformity and who could climb the ladder fastest instead of the power that is generated from dreaming out those diversity of talents, the unique paths of purpose, love and transformation that are already alive within. To dream or not to dream—*that* is the real question."

Like I said, I didn't need any more convincing as far as my willingness was concerned. My "want-to" was off the charts. It was my know-how and, well, perhaps my courage that still needed a little prodding.

"Will, I understand your trepidations, and the tension you feel between desire and action. It's a line that only you can cross, one that many struggle with. No life, politician or family member can, or will, do it for you. Only you can stare the wolves in the face and let them know that you will not be pastured for slaughter. It's not by voice but by steady, persevering, consistent action.

That part takes the most courage. Fear is a bully of intimidation just waiting to be stood up to, stared down, and stepped past. He belongs in the rearview mirror. You might feel like you get a couple bloody noses standing up to him, but he will ultimately pay the higher price as you walk on by. Courage comes when you allow the fire in your heart to outgrow the demons you've let stand in front of you, and stay the course. Come on, follow me this way."

We began walking northeast, towards more of the monuments. Well, I began walking, Founder was usually a couple bursts of flight ahead of me. But he always circled back around patiently.

We approached the monument of Abraham Lincoln. I was astonished. The sheer size of it made me feel like I was dreaming—which of course, I was, having never actually been to D.C. I didn't know how I'd remember it when awake. Could I say that I visited it now? Or was it a dream? Or, maybe, it was both. Maybe dreams aren't some idyllic fantasy, maybe they can become reality, or even greater than.

"That, Will, was one of the most profound statements I have ever heard. Not just from you, but words I believe all of us can live by. It can be both, and yes, your dreams can become a reality far greater than the foundation you originally dream from. My question to you is, do you really believe it?"

"Well, Founder, *that* is one of the most profound questions I have heard," I said with a laugh, poking back at him. However, it really was a tough question that now aimed unrelentingly at my heart. "I don't know. I don't know if I believe it, but I want to."

"That's enough for me, Will, and much more than many others will put on the table. Where we stand now is the very place Dr. Martin Luther King Jr. gave his famous speech. Truly, it was more of a declaration. Few of us have the courage to make—let alone live—such declarations. But you can, Will, you can. Especially when you remember, and believe, that actions speak louder than words. You may or may not stand on this mall or another podium one day to declare such a passionate, world-changing speech. But, you can live such a speech every day of your life and speak to everyone who even *might* be watching."

"Will, today is the day that dream begins for you. Come and stand here. This is where Dr. King stood." I trembled at Founder's words. It hardly felt possible, especially as my understanding and respect for Dr. King grew so loud in my heart. "Will, tell me—*tell the world*— what is your dream? What dream do you have? Better yet, what dream has *you*?"

I thought I was trembling before, but now, my knees were clearly knocking. I had never been put so on the spot before, and with the gravity of such a life as Dr. King's breathing down my neck. I didn't know where to start. I mean, my mom and dad wouldn't have even asked me half of such a loaded question. And now Founder wanted me to answer *that*, and *here*? I didn't think I was ready.

Sure, I remember having dreams as a kid. I wanted to be a professional athlete. I wanted to be rich. I wanted to be a doctor, and at one point I wanted to be recruited by superheroes for their team. Don't ask. But this was a different kind of dream Founder was asking for—*the real kind*—the kind that matter. Did I truly have one? And even if I did, did I actually believe in its possibility? I knew I might want its possibility, but I didn't know if I believed. Belief is a scary subject, and I don't always know if I want to put myself out there like that. What if it doesn't work? What if I'm wrong? What if….

"Will, that's fear talking, not you. It's the "what if's" of life the wolves have worked so hard to construct. You can't think like that if you're ever going to live anything of substance. Life of such promise doesn't come because it's easy, or free, but because you seize such freedom."

I shook my head as if I could actually rid such fearful persuasions from my thoughts. I didn't know if I really could, but it was worth a try. Then I started over. I stepped into the spot Founder had pointed to and looked down at my own shadow, the only darkness on the sun-drenched mall of white walled concrete.

"I…uh, uh, IIII…I have a dream?" I spoke aloud as

if I had a question, surely not a statement. Founder looked at me with that look in his eyes, a look like my parents had given me once or twice—that look that said "You're crazy if you think I'm gonna let you get away with *that*!" Obviously not what Founder had envisioned, and I sure hoped I wasn't dreaming in questions either. But it was hard, way harder than I thought. There wasn't even a single soul there but Founder, and I still struggled to stand tall and speak out my dream with conviction. There was a confidence I was missing, not just in myself, but a confidence in my own freedom to boldly dream.

"Founder," I interrupted my own task, "I don't know what my dream is. I feel it, but I don't know it right now. For me—*this*—these dreams with you, they are my dream. This is the world I've been hoping to live in—or escape to I guess. This is the only 'more' that I know right now."

Founder looked at me and let out a bit of a sigh. He seemed disappointed, but also a little bit like he understood. He stood completely still just looking at me. It was hard to take. But I didn't know what more to speak out.

"Soon enough, Will, you will understand; right now this is not so much about the words you speak as much as it is the courage to actually live free again. The freedom you live is much greater than any freedom you can possess. Your dream is secondary to your courage because no dream, no matter how noble, can ever be vivid enough to actually wake people up without such courage. Dr. King stood here not because he had a perfect dream, but because he was courageous enough to live and walk through the imperfect—in himself and the world around him. Courage amplifies such a dream, and makes the words that accompany your dream that much more powerful. I don't fault you, Will, for not knowing your dream just yet, it's just that I so badly want you to have the courage—and the freedom—to believe."

****

I didn't have a dream at that point, but I knew I got something from our time on the National Mall. I had finally understood the true purpose of our nighttime journeys together. And I was beginning to understand more about myself as well, parts of me that had been asleep for years. There was something more that was birthing, a greater dream, but before the world could hear it I had to learn to pioneer its terrain inside myself, no easy task to be sure. Dr. King had what I wanted—*the courage to believe.* I learned that hope wasn't free after all, for it carries the price of courage.

Chapter 9:
The Fifth Dream:
The River & A Friend

"Two roads diverged in a wood and I—I took the one less traveled by, and that made all the difference."
- Robert Frost

"Welcome to the Oregon Trail," Founder said robustly. We were walking through the woods and I couldn't stop my head from turning side to side, taking in the vast treasures of this wilderness, so much so I was surprised I hadn't tripped for lack of paying attention. It was like being in another world. With the towering trees, the deep greens, and the rich soil. Who knew dirt could hold such esteem? In all our camping, I had never seen the woods like this. Or perhaps, more fittingly, maybe the woods had never seen me like this, with a deeper appreciation for their majesty. I felt like I was in a storybook, with kingdom all around me. Though I wasn't actually in a fairytale, I was sure Founder had some new story for me, and I was more than happy to listen.

"The Oregon Trail, huh? I've heard of the video game, but didn't know it was a real place."

Founder snuffed with disgust.

"Video game culture? Really, Will? Does that even belong in the same sentence as this?" Founder asked as he swooped up in the air flipping a loop de loop through the freedom of the air.

I was sure he just answered his own question, that is, if he was really asking a question at all. "The Oregon Trail is the path of true pioneers, the ones your culture was ultimately built off of. They had a pioneering spirit about them that was never meant to die. They risked life for the sake of life. They lived into the new before anyone could identify it. They were more like shepherds than sheep, and if anyone knew the ways of the wolves, it was the pioneers. But they didn't just avoid the culture of wolves; they defied it with every pioneering step onto new fertile ground, seeing this land for what it could be in the hands of a people willing to live the river life. Now, the culture they created as pioneers has been sustained not as a pioneering, life-giving river but as a culture of ponds. The pioneering spirit birthed the American dream, until too many feared loss more than true freedom and gave their herd to be led by wolves. The wolves were once held back because of such a pioneering spirit, but without such a faith for the impossible the wolves slowly started to move in to steal even that which would be notoriously possible. The pioneers kept moving forward in their hope, never stagnant, always stewarding their gain towards something more, never hoarding the pleasures of this world but rather using them for fuel. A stagnant people is an easy target for the wolves, but timely movement produces more new life."

As he spoke, one thing in particular stood out to me as especially unusual, or perhaps intriguing.

"River life?" I asked. "What is that? What kind of life does the river represent?"

"Will, you are developing a great new aptitude for the things of my world, that's for sure. You hit the nail on the head, and that's exactly where we are going; to see if we can drive that nail a little deeper."

"To the river?" I asked.

"Yes, there's someone I want you to meet, and if you take the time to listen, the river itself has a lot to say and teach. The river is the ultimate pioneer. If you want to take back the pioneering spirit that confounds the wolves you and your family are feeling, *learn the river*. For the river lives and moves and breathes—wherever it goes. It gives life while also taking new ground. The river is the picture of the path of a pioneer. It may look unsafe in its twists, turns and the varying seasons and terrain it unpredictably encounters moving forward, but when you are found in the river there is not a safer place on earth.

"The wolves stay far from there, and us eagles find it to be some of the most hospitable life there is, full of the best fresh salmon I could ask for, more adventure and reward in such. It is not just a place, it's a lifestyle, a culture of life that never stops breathing, that allows those who are hurting and dying for refreshment to take a deep breath or drink. Too many people trade the river's appearance of insecurity and unpredictability while looking for ponds of assurance to fill the insecurity deep within their own lives and thoughts. One takes new ground all around you, and the other takes away ground from within you. One is a culture of pioneers, and the other a culture of wolves. The way of the river is not always easy, but rest assured that over the long haul, it is the most secure. It is what your nation was founded upon, and what it must return to if they will ever learn to dream, again."

The pine needles crunched under my feet as we walked, reminding me of some of the few old, good memories I had with my family, when life was still present during those fall hikes. We never made it up to the peaks of perspective per se, but at least we were on the right track. Nature abounded here, and reminded me how much creation had to offer. Various animals surrounded us, and birds—even eagles such as Founder—soared high overhead. How I wished I could hear their loud ongoing conversations the way I could hear Founder. I assumed that I could learn much, if I could only still myself long enough to listen. Imagine their perspective on what had become the life we lived. They knew more about the wolf culture that had found its way out to inhabit suburbs and cities such as mine, as the wolves moved to where deception could more freely abound, and be more easily disguised. These animals had known those tricks for generations, and had prevailed. What I wasn't sure of though, knowing the fading hope that was still back home, was whether we could survive the life we had fallen into. Looking up at the birds, I wished for their wings so as to simply rise above it all. And in reality, I knew I was slowly getting my wings day-by-day, and change-by-change.

I heard the river moving nearby, so we had to be close. Suddenly, I felt a tapping on the back of my knee. I jumped two feet forward nearly scared out of my boots and turned to look back. It obviously wasn't Founder as he was still circling very low overhead. I furrowed my brow at the sight of his little furry coat and twitching little nose, apparently sniffing me out for an introduction.

"Her!" Founder interjected.

"She's a her," he said again, making sure I wouldn't offend. She stood before me, a small beaver covered head to toe in river water that made her shine unusually. Her presence was wildly soothing, if not so oddly out of place. But then again, I was more the one who was out of place, though hopefully not for much longer.

"Hi!" she spoke up.

I was taken off-guard as she reached out her paw politely. I had many conversations with Founder, but I was still startled to be beginning one with this new friend.

"I'm Peace," she said with a bit of a glow. "I live in the river. Founder is an old friend of mine. He asked me to join you both today."

Founder swooped down to stand by our sides. He smiled ear to ear. "Peace can, and will guide you through the river far better than I could. I come to the river often, but I still live in the skies. But if anyone knows the river life and all it has to offer, it is Peace. She knows what it takes to live in the culture that a river creates, and better yet, Peace knows how not only to survive in such unchartered waters, but how to thrive there."

She smiled brightly, very unassuming and sweet spirited.

"Let's go," she said in a calm but firm voice. "We're very close."

It was only a hundred yards or so before we reached the bank of the river. "Ahhh." Peace basked in the river's presence, like she hadn't been there in weeks.

You wouldn't have known that she had scurried out of the river less than a minute before tapping on my knee. Founder swooped down to our side.

"Peace loves the river and is found there far more than in tranquil ponds. She builds her house on the river and rarely strays very far. If you want to find Peace, always start in the river. Sight might show you certain misconceptions of the river life, but Peace can calm all those. She abides in rapids that cannot touch her as she tames even the mightiest of swells and turns a pioneer's path into her home. Listen to her, follow her, and wherever you go in the river; you can take Peace with you. She won't leave you for as long as you abide with her. She is the one traveling companion that makes the impossibilities of the river possible."

Peace jumped into the river like an overjoyed child.

"C'mon!" she said.

She was a creature of few words, but Peace always seemed to carry a certain joy and an inexplicably pure happiness. She was undaunted to the pressures of the water and she didn't seem even the slightest bit allured to the banks on either side. They were just a means to carve out the river life she loved. Just watching her, I realized that was how I wanted my life to look, an allure that didn't make much sense in practicality, but an undercurrent that I wanted to have flowing through my life too. To know Peace, already, was to know the kind of joy that seemed to be fading from my house and life. A joy I was now beginning to crave in my dreams. I had been taught to dream of success, and found no joy. But Peace, she ran down the unpredictability of the river like there was no greater joy to be found. I wonder if that's how those Pioneers once felt? They sought the peace of a new path because they knew there was more joy to be had. I wonder what their dreams were, and I doubted my life reflected what they once pioneered with sweat and blood. But Peace, this overflowing little Beaver seemed to know well everything they paid for. I hoped that some day, I might as well.

"Go with her Will," Founder spoke up, waking me from my thoughts. I looked at him like he must be crazy. The river looked cold, was full of rocks, and I had never simply jumped into a river before.

"Well, that's fine then," Founder stated bluntly. "But if you want to be with Peace, eventually you're going to have to jump in and shake it off. Fear can only hold you so long as you allow it to. Sheep are frightened easily, you must overcome your fears with each new step, and sometimes, a good and unexpected splash is required!"

I wasn't sure if I was afraid, or thought I was above playing in the water, but maybe I just had a hard time admitting it to myself.

"Peace will not battle your fears for you. But she will lead you far enough away from them that it is hard to remember what you were afraid of in the first place. It's ironic, because usually fear is only a lie, a shadow that is puffed up for intimidation sake. Step through your shadow, and you might just splash into the life you've been dreaming of."

I looked at Founder. Then back at Peace. I glanced back at Founder one more time with a nervous smirk starting to arise, and then I jumped.

"Wooohooo!" I yelled. Peace met me immediately in the water and started splashing me with the smacking of her tail, covering me head to toe by the time she was done, while the water seemed to dance in slow motion all around us. Like a joyous water fight, it seemed the river must have been filled with something other than your standard H2O—very euphoric—without the weightiness or burdens I usually felt trampling on my heart. It became something of a coating I hadn't known before, or at least that I hadn't recognized. It was simple, almost childlike.

"The river is an unusual path, and its full of nutrients that other terrain just can't give you," Founder spoke up.

Peace turned back around from splashing me and joined in as well. "With each passing year I have seen fewer and fewer walk this trail. Few know how to walk on water," she laughed, "and even more envy the security of the bank. But you can't cash in on the river by staying near the bank, you must absorb the culture the river brings and make its movement your foundation, while learning to trust the sort of water that lives inside. But, that's enough talk, let's have some fun!" She certainly was eager, and I have to admit, it was quite contagious.

"Is it alright if I call you Will?" Peace asked, so gentle and polite.

"Of course you can. But may I ask, where exactly are we headed?"

"So many people are afraid of river life and the tension one must navigate in between the banks of certainty. They want to live this way, or that way, this extreme, or that extreme, black or white—always a known quantity, rarely learning to trust the power of the river. Most say the river is dangerous and irresponsible. It curves and turns and sometimes it even doubles back to find the right path. It slows its pace at times, but then it picks up again quickly. It is always moving, but because of such movement its waters are beyond reproach in their purity, and very refreshing to the soul. Sure, most of its terrain is unchartered, and typically people are taught to prefer walking a paved, comfortable, more sure path. People seem to prefer man-made structures, such as ponds. But to me, a pond feels more like sitting in year old bath water. The view of the river is much like a pioneer, while the pond, well, it looks and lives a lot like your culture does today, accumulating something sure, but in its own stagnancy."

"How so?" I asked curiously, not entirely tracking yet. "I mean, I understand the beauty and joy of the river as just that, a river. That's what finally propelled me when I jumped in to join you, right Peace? But I don't necessarily understand it within my culture."

"You jumped into this river," Peace responded giddily while pointing at her home. "But you need to learn how to jump in and live out *that river.*" Peace finished while pointing to the conviction I was not so obviously feeling in my heart.

I wasn't sure of the definition she seemed to know so well, but something about what she said, even without saying much struck a massive cord in me. It was like something inside me that had been powered off for years was suddenly turned on, a hidden option revealed. Peace truly was a pioneer of the river and something told me she was helping to pioneer a rushing rapid within me as well.

"Will, the river in you is the unique path rarely walked, a path that doesn't get walked on by many sheep—who hate to get wet by the way—and such a path kind of breaks the box of what is considered progress in life. Many see progress as building up and growing out rather than moving forward to take and occupy new ground, while giving life to so much creation, and to do so with joy and freedom. New isn't always safe, and surely not predictable, but Will, there is a purpose inside you that wants to pioneer and impact the world. There is value in you that wants its place, which is too often bartered for deeper ponds. It's up to you whether you will live it out for the rest to drink of. That river of purpose doesn't often fit in the land it currently resides because it is designed to be unique and lead others into new territory; territory that many don't yet know is possible. That's how the founders of your country and the pioneers began the culture you now live. Their lives looked more like rivers, and they left the ponds of their past to bring such rich river waters to you. I guess the question is, will you learn to do the same?"

I thought back through various history classes in school. In that instant I already wished I had paid better attention and definitely would from that point forward. But I thought about the stories I did remember, the stories of leaders who fought for a freedom they believed was inside them long before such freedom existed, that which began in their spirits long before it made manifest in their laws. Leaders who came to another world before there were structures or institution in place, and leaders who pioneered out west from their original landing point; just like Peace and Founder were discussing before, they were pioneers who kept moving forward like a river, never growing stagnant in their pursuit. I didn't see many people live that way now. I didn't live that way—yet.

Peace started walking forward, but began to veer and climb out of the river. "Let's go Will, we want to show you the pond now."

Founder was overhead joining us and leading the way. I was curious to see the difference. Peace didn't have her usual bounce while she scurried, a little more melancholy and dutiful, almost sad. She reached up and grabbed my hand, clearly wanting to stay with me. I watched Founder who was as focused as ever. He appeared in countenance as if he could already see the pond we were headed for, bracing for its culture. We emerged from the bank of the river, over a slight hill, and just as we came out of the thinning trees, *there it was.*

"It's beautiful," I said aloud, not even realizing it, but quickly taken without thought. I was drawn to the sight immediately. The still waters were captivating from far off where we still stood. I could sense a peace that was calling to me, loudly, wooing me into its overt desire. I couldn't take my eyes off its offering. It was set down in the valley and the water looked no different from that of the river, except maybe more beautiful and the fact it was serene and still instead of moving. The sun reflected off it in so many ways, unique colors I hadn't seen in the river. I saw houses all around the pond that had been constructed for living; unlike the ruggedness of the river everything here seemed so explained and understandable. I felt a little more peace, like I was in my own comfort zone, somewhere that didn't leave me feeling so new.

I could hear Founder staying with me in step, flapping his wings overhead, never leaving me as I now led our momentum closer towards the pond. I passed a number of animals on my way; ducks, frogs, turtles, and as I approached the pond itself I even saw some *shee...*I stopped myself. What was I thinking? How did I not notice?

"Sheep?" I cried.

"Founder, where are we? And, where, where is Peace?" I asked, looking around for her frantically.

"You traded her away for another peace," he said sternly, obviously none too pleased.

"Wha, why didn't you stop me then?" I asked him back, with a hint of frustration.

"You didn't ask," Founder said. "You were so caught up in what you were seeing you lost the new vision you were living by, trading it in for the old and comfortable wiles of the wolves. It is an easy and common thing to do, especially when near the pond. You traded the real Peace you abide by while walking in your purpose for an external peace, the false peace that you get from being comfortable. The pond has the allure of peace and comfort, but it is very much counterfeit, a mask for stagnancy and a harvest field for the wolves."

I almost forgot what interrupted me in the first place, the sheep.

"Those are wolves, right Founder?" I asked, trying to shake myself out of it, blinking incessantly while attempting to truly see again. My vision blurred for a second, then refocused. There they were, occupying all the structures all around the pond, dens of wolves, and in sheep's clothing no less, worn wool that certainly wasn't growing having been scalped from those led into deception, and worn by the wolves for a sheepish version of power, manipulation and control. I quickly ran back up to the top of the hill and stopped at the edge of the trees as Founder joined me.

"I want Peace back!" I declared, somewhat to myself, mostly towards Founder, my head on a swivel, frantically looking side to side for where she might still be waiting.

"You can have her again, but that is your choice, and such choice is only inside you and the priorities, and vision, that you choose one on top of another. Before you choose, first, I want you to look further into the pond with me. You can't just know the warnings, you have to understand the nature of the lies because they come in all sorts of ways and forms."

"Will, the pond is filled with the same water as the river and much can be done with it. But, the biggest issue of such institution is it is built around comfort, security, and false peace. All those are masks for stagnancy, and do you know what happens to stagnant water, Will?"

I dared not answer the question, not sure whether it

was a trick question or not.

"You know the answer Will, there is no trick from me, only from the pond. See, a pond is a large, long-standing trap of its own. A pond seems more secure. It seems more sustainable. The pond has the appearance of results and life you can see and build upon, even measure the depth of, and count it's accumulated fish and gathered—but not grown—life that is around it but not connected to it. It possesses trees it can call its own, and much more. Essentially, the pond seems more guaranteed. However, that is not all the pond guarantees. The pond also possesses the guarantee that all stagnant water carries in that it will no doubt grow fungus, bacteria and disease. The very same water from the river when given out of a stagnant structure rather than a forward moving one actually breeds disease over the long term instead of breeding life. That's also why you saw so many new colors. Those weren't natural but manufactured through chemicals. The pond water is on life support, and lives off of chemicals so sheep still think it is water, rather than seeing its true sludge."

"In the short term it is much more comfortable and seems more peaceful. But over the long haul, you will have traded your peace and purpose with the river for a pond that is polluted, which slowly pollutes many areas of your own life. Just because it is water doesn't mean it is river water. One gives life to all it touches, the other breeds disease and death through desires of comfort and self. Pioneers didn't give up their comfort just so you could live in the lies they walked away from. They weren't trying simply to give you and all the generations after them something to possess, they were showing you a different way to live. I wonder if your culture has traded its freedom of living for freedom of possessing? Aim for the first, you get the second thrown in. Aim for the second, eventually, you'll get neither."

Before he could finish the last word Founder was already heading back towards the river, obviously assuming I would be joining him. And I did. He flew anxiously in front of me, though not so far for me to lose vision of him. We came to the river again and he swooped down upon a rock next to Peace, who was grinning ear to ear, waiting earnestly with hope for my return.

"You're back!" She shouted. "I was worried you had been taken by the pond again."

"I was," I responded. "But Founder helped me find my vision again. I'm sorry I left you, Peace. Please forgive me. I just lost sight for a moment of how different and real you genuinely are, and how special your river-led life really is. I have a lot to learn if I'm going to stay on such a rugged, but rustling path."

"No worries," she said without any begrudging tone at all. "I'm just ready to dive into the adventures of your purpose with you and see where the river leads!"

I couldn't help but chuckle at her. What a funny, but true, creature. Peace would be my traveling companion upon this river. I looked down at my own heart this time, knowing that is where the river begins, seeing now that I simply had to get past the wooded dam of my own old thoughts and perspectives, beyond my comforts and fears, and trust the river.

"That's ok," Peace chimed in to my thoughts, much like Founder often did. "That's what I'm here for!" And from that point on I knew: to pioneer my purpose in life, this new friend Peace would be the one to lead me, but I could only find her in the river; and I had to learn to live there as well.

Chapter 10:
The Sixth Dream: Consumed

"Conformity is the jailer of freedom and the enemy of growth." - John F. Kennedy

I was a little perplexed as to where we landed this time. We were in what looked like an old, small town. It was plain, but there was a fullness, or richness, that I had never experienced anywhere else. It looked like an early to mid 1900's version of the suburbs, though I don't suppose there was anything so suburban back then. I stood on a neighborhood corner in between a street of houses and a row of shops, across from an empty field. People were walking all around me. There were fewer cars, but more neighbors than I had ever seen. I knew people existed like this and all, but these, they, everyone was actually very neighborly, almost seemed foreign to what I had become used to.

Where I had felt unseen in other dreams, in this place it seemed that not only did everyone see me, they all knew me by name as well. They most certainly knew one another. This felt like more of a dream than any of the adventures Founder had led me on, almost eerie, but quite pleasant. I don't know if I had ever used that word before to describe anything to be honest. But, it was, the town and everyone within it was really very pleasant.

They dressed very plain; muted colors, black, navy and but a few patterns painted across their modest clothes. Excessive use of fabric it seemed compared to how I was used to people dressing—most of who celebrated skin more than thread. I didn't have a fashion preference per se, but life just looked very different. I couldn't quite understand where we were but I liked the spirit of it, felt like the missing piece from back home. Yeah, home had a lot of other advances compared to this place, and at times I might have even referred to life such as this as boring, or even lame. But there was something that grabbed me. A quality about this place stuck out like cherries in a pie, an easy analogy with the smells that were dancing in my direction. In fact, the way I was seeing it lately my modern life was more like the a la mode that might as well be melting away at the heat of accompanying pressures—but this was the pie.

I saw that Founder was perched up in the old tree overhead. He was a good twenty feet up, which wouldn't be possible in most neighborhoods these days. Founder seemed to be handling the neighborhood the same as me, quiet and observant. I don't think I had ever watched people so closely. There was intentionality to the way things seemed to work—so seamlessly—and the people interacted effortlessly, dominated by kindness, almost as if they had no masks with anything to hide at all. I'm sure that wasn't the case, but it sure felt like a lot less than I was accustomed to.

Founder dropped down with wings spread to slow his landing. Still looking around, it was like we were on an island and the angel of suburbs past had swept me away into a land where soda hadn't yet replaced a tall glass of cold milk. And to be sure, Founder was my angel.

"I'm no angel, Will," Founder chuckled. "But we are going on a venture similar to the one old Scrooge fell into that night, albeit a little bit different. What do you think of this town? How does it feel to you?"

"I guess it feels pretty warm. I don't just mean the temperature is increased, but there is almost an invitation of warmth all around me jumping right off everyone, kind of weird actually. To tell you the truth, I'm quite curious as to how they can see me here anyway, and even more how they know my name? I definitely would have thought a place like this would have been way too old fashioned for me, so it's surprising to say that I'm actually enjoying it more each minute. There's a purity here I haven't really tasted before, a simplicity that doesn't come across as simple, *but real.* It kind of makes me think of a home-cooked meal. I've had more than my fair share of frozen dinners—even more fast food—but this place feels like the crock-pot I always smelled simmering at Grandma's when I was really young. I didn't think much of it then, and I don't even think I knew that I missed it until now—*here.*"

"Indeed, Will. I can smell the same thing. Let's cross the street to that open field and see it from a different perspective. As we've discussed before, there's so much right under your nose that you can learn just by seeing from a different vantage point."

We began to cross the street and I was halfway looking for the flashing sign to lead us until I remembered where we were. A milk truck zipped by; I could hear the bottles clanking. The house adjacent to the field we were walking towards was full of laughter, kids running through the yard, leaping through sprays of water and chasing one another with buckets full. I really envied them. I missed, or, I suppose I wanted those days that I never really had. I grew up with computers more than sprinklers, video games instead of football or kick the can in the streets. There was something deep within me that latched onto their laughter and wanted to make it my own.

Founder was fifteen yards or so ahead perched on a

bench in the field. No doubt a field that must have gotten lots of use from the neighborhood. I stepped up the curb and onto the sidewalk, but within that one step everything changed. My mouth dropped and tears almost followed. I didn't know what happened—to my friend or this neighborhood. The field was not a field anymore, and Founder was no more than a statue of bronze that welcomed shoppers into the mall. "Mall?" I spoke out loud—very loud. "What is this place?" I ran over to Founder, petting his head feathers hoping to wake him up while others walked by me staring, probably hoping the crazy person I appeared to be petting the statue wouldn't follow them instead. They obviously saw me, but there was no warmth whatsoever and I was almost certain they didn't know my name anymore.

I flipped around to look back at the neighborhood. Most of the homes were gone. The smells of pie were replaced by the smell of, well, nothing. And the laughs of the kids couldn't be heard under all the sounds of ongoing construction. They were probably all in the mall anyway. The street I had just crossed was no neighborhood road anymore but three lanes of traffic and lights. The old shops were gone, likely for an extra lane and I don't even know if milk existed anymore from the looks of all the other drink ads. But to be honest, this looked more like home to me so I don't know why I was so upset.

I had only been in the other neighborhood for a

matter of minutes, well under an hour. *But I missed it.* For the first time, I wasn't used to this life anymore after getting a taste of something so pure. I missed Founder too. His large soaring wings had been relegated to molded art; a fixture of what once was all squeezed into a small and empty memorial of such. Was he inside the statue? Was he *in* the mall? I turned in circles as if I was on a moving podium, a little confused and not quite feeling like I was living any kind of dream anymore, but snatched back into the reality I longed to see heartily upgraded. Felt very lonely around here, a loneliness that couldn't be filled by my iPod, video games or anything else. The current look was so familiar, but I didn't know what to do anymore. So I went inside the mall.

Just like the mall back home, this one had all the brands and fixtures. It had all the top-notch shops, brand name clothes and sky-high prices from what I could tell. But I wasn't there to shop. When awake back home, I often begged Mom for money to go along with a trip to the mall. Couldn't have been further from my mind now. I wanted what I had, that glimpse of a life that felt like it was something fulfilled. Most of all I wanted Founder, even if it meant a scavenger hunt through this museum of consumerism.

However, I decided not to rush. Founder had a different way of doing things and new ways of teaching me. I tried to resist my natural instincts so I could slow my mind down and think like Founder might. What is this place? What is its purpose? Where might Founder be hidden—or buried? It almost felt funny to find no treasure in this mall opportunity, instead rummaging through its in-your-face nature to find what might be naturally underneath. Even the smell put me off, I don't know what it was but a headache was quickly coming on. That little town had to be in here somewhere; it couldn't just disappear. Though I knew I wasn't likely to find the town until I could first locate Founder.

Instead of plowing through the mall or even slowly going forward I found what I deemed to be the highest bird's eye view in the place. I thought if I could look at everything from a higher perspective—rather than just my perspective—that I'd see far more. The peak of perspective had shown me as much. It was time to put it to use on my own.

From this viewing point it seemed like everything and everyone slowed down a little. It was probably just for not being smack in the middle of the coming and going, the buying and competing. I had never liked that part anyway. Probably because I never much felt like I could compete or even come close to measure up. This time, it was for the right reasons and minus the wrong attitude. Either way, things were slowing down for me from up here.

I scanned the walkways of the mall up and down, shop after shop. There was little that looked natural, even most of the plants appeared to be fake. There must have been some metaphor built into that, I thought with a laugh. The fountain ahead was but recycled water, certainly not from a river and perhaps even worse than a pond.

That's when it hit me. I knew how to unearth Founder. I had to think in layers to get there, but I was sure I'd find him somewhere at the bottom of such. If I wanted to find Founder I had to go to the root of what might be suffocating the freedom of his wings—the culture of wolves. But they wouldn't present themselves as wolves here. So, if I wanted to find the wolves I had to follow the sheep. And if I were to follow the sheep I'd have to jump right back into the flow of the mall, but make sure I kept a different, higher perspective in the process. I was going shopping, but not to buy my typical desires—though I had many—this time I was going to buy-back the culture I had lost.

I followed shopper after shopper through one store, then another. Nothing! I was beginning to get discouraged when something occurred to me; Founder was everywhere. He was just being used differently. They didn't know him like I did. They knew him as their right to gain and consume. I assume that's why he'd been relegated to a statue outside, they had memorialized what he and his natural freedom could mean to culture for the sake of superficial gain. Consumerism had consumed him, *consumed us*. The living parts of Founder had been devoured by how we abused our rights. Shopping and consumerism wasn't wrong I didn't think; it's just how it was being used. Certainly that was what happened to the town as well, and the crock-pot feel that I would rather consume instead. I had experienced all of this before and every time it left me empty and coming back for more. Founder, and the town that was before us on the other side of the street was one of the first things I could remember that actually made me feel full.

I rushed outside to the statue of Founder and there he was, upright and living again on top of the statue that had seemed to contain him before—with the entire town restored behind him. The mall was still oddly present, so the field obviously had not returned either but Founder was alive and breathing again. Cultures could not have conflicted any more had they been on opposite sides of the world. We had crossed to the other side, and purposefully so. Founder had clearly led me into that one knowing full well his statuesque destiny. Sometimes I just wished he'd warn me of these potholes in our journey in advance. Then again, I likely wouldn't let it digest far enough simply being told without tasting it for myself.

"Will," he said, "Can't you see how divided culture has become? The division isn't in the differences of culture, but of freedom. Society is divided between true and false forms of freedom. It is those who choose to see as you just have that will rebuild *this* town and culture, one step at a time. Change like this occurs when those like you stand up to conformity. Most are too consumed by the tricks of the wolves to hunger for something more, but you have learned well. Each person who chooses courage over conformity, and change over what's become commonplace, they begin to pave the path for another to live likewise. Most try to do it on a big, broad, political scale. That rarely works anymore. There is too much money in conformity, and tricks of the wolves to make us comfortable there. Many have tried to stand and be their own example but became discouraged because of the adversity pond culture brings upon the river life. Will, persevere with the river and you will continue to find Peace there. The longer you abide with Peace, the more she will join you. The river will get broader by the day—one life at a time."

"Thanks for finding me, Will. It only takes one who will choose to believe. I hate being a statue or an emblem more than you know. I've learned my lessons from it. But I can use such a position to look for those like you, the emerging, and re-emerging ones who have neither conformed, nor grown bitter. You don't have to be perfect, but you do have to spread your wings. Don't hide them underneath what you can buy in the mall, nor let such freedom be contained in bronze or candy coated memoriam, rather, let them follow you into the skies where you are out of the way of the food chain and ready to dream, again. When you spread your wings, you spread me!"

****

I didn't wake up that day with a dislike for malls or consumerism. That's an easy way out, and very unproductive from what I had seen. No, I woke up with brighter eyes and a fuller stomach. Mom could make frozen meals all she wanted but from now on, in life, I decided to eat what Grandma used to cook in the crock-pot. I liked that people cared to know my name and I wanted to belong to a culture where such life was restored, mixed with the advances of modern culture. This feeling was only beginning to stir in me, but I knew that I had been consumed for long enough already. Now, the possibility of real food was on the table and it was my turn to eat, maybe even invite others and give them vision again for a home-cooked meal.

Chapter 11:
The Seventh Dream:
Yellowstone

"I sustain myself with the love of family."
- Maya Angelou

"Will, I'd like you to meet your new traveling companion."

Founder made his newest introduction while perched up on the high back of a towering horse. I had never seen a horse with the likes of his stature. It wasn't just his height, but also the strength and presence he held, sturdy like the reverent trees just behind him. The powerful definition of each and every muscle, and yet a grace so tangible one would have thought him to be royalty if not for his plain, every day attire—or lack thereof.

"Hello!" I said with a grin.

The horse immediately dropped to a knee—or several—while blustering out in a distinguished tone, "Nnneeeiigghhhhhh." But that was it. There were no words, or was I just not hearing them, I wondered. After learning to see so differently, and recently meeting Peace, I fully anticipated his bluster to pronounce more than a few syllables.

"He is not a talking horse," Founder clued me in. "But that doesn't subtract from his incredible nature that you first perceived. His name is Honor, and you must learn to ride him through our newest endeavor. Without Honor, you will not be able to understand the journey ahead. Honor, though a word often associated with royal or older cultures, is too frequently unheard of in the culture you now stem from. He will carry you into places you could not otherwise go, and he will allow you to venture in and out of those places—even the difficult ones—unscathed. He is friend of the greatest of pioneers, especially those to come, hopefully you will be able to bring him forward into and for their dream journey's as well."

"I know others in your culture have now mostly abandoned traveling by him, switching to other means of advancement, but Honor is a true friend, kind and giving, strong and secure. He will lead you forward from now on as much as you will let him, taking you by foot as I join you by air."

Honor was still kneeling down before me. "He is

awaiting your permission, for him Honor is not just a name."

"Thank you, Honor," I said with a nod. I wasn't all that familiar with the ways of a horse. He arose strongly, with a resolute gentleness that was unmoved, but very moving for me. His appearance and mannerisms were almost contradictory it seemed. He was so powerful, yet so gentle, highly esteemed, and yet giving. His height towered above me, and probably many others—horses and people—yet he bowed low and almost made me feel like a king. It was overwhelming, but good it seemed. He inspired me without words.

However, I had little to no experience riding horses and I didn't see a saddle anywhere around us. Knowing my times with Founder, I assumed this was not going to be a deterrent, a sentiment Founder loudly echoed. "You don't need a saddle," he spoke as if rolling his eyes, but that was never Founder's way, more of a playful, expectant tone. "The more you are one with Honor, the better off you will be moving forward. In fact, it would be hard to make the most of this opportunity while on a saddle. As you ride Honor you need to feel his every movement, his lead, his give, his surrender and the strength of his positions and direction. He will give you perspective when you need it, take you closer when you should advance and will pull you back when he sees fit. You will not so much be leading Honor with controlling reigns as much as Honor will be leading you."

I trusted Founder enough by now to let go on this one. The giant horse sidled up to me closely, and again lowered himself to his knees. Founder glanced at me, an obvious direction as to what I was supposed to do—so I hopped on. I tried to be careful when climbing aboard. The horse's value for me only gave me even greater esteem for him, as well as Founder, if that was even possible. He waited until I was nestled in to the crook of his back and suddenly arose like a building rising up in one swift, smooth fashion.

"Where are we, Founder?"

"We're at Yellowstone," he responded with special sentiment now easily found in his tone.

"Yellowstone? You mean, like the park?" I asked.

"Park? Yes, well, I guess some might call it that now. However, I have always known it in a very different way." He grinned, and I saw that twinkle in his eye again. With Founder, something was always up. This time was no different.

"C'mon Will, this is a wonderful place and it's treasures are well beyond words, to me at least. Treasure often lies in the eye of the beholder, but it's hard to state that much anymore knowing the condition of today's vision and perspective. But hopefully such will soon be redeemed."

I had loved my times with Founder up until now,

and had nothing negative to say. But this was a different sort of excitement, a deeper connection to something, or so I sensed. Founder's anticipation was clear, clear enough to be my lens as well. His joy was fun to witness and even generated a measure of unknown excitement in me that I'd kept at bay for a long time, the kind of emotion you're almost afraid to have because you don't want to get your hopes up and once again become that heaping pile of disappointment. But Founder's genuine appreciation for this place gave me the assurance that my own would not be misplaced either. I wished I could be around more of such people, or such eagles, for that matter.

Honor began to trot forward slowly, allowing me to get my bearings. And Founder could hardly contain himself watching us move so slowly. He looked backwards and down at us like Honor and I were *that* car, clearly hindering the entire flow of traffic. I had never seen impatience in Founder before, a trait that actually seemed to carry him further and faster.

His patience must have fully run its course at that moment. Out of pure joy, he literally leapt, if that's even possible already in mid-air, and flew straight up like he was shot out of a cannon. It looked like he went to the top of the world in mere seconds, then swooped down to meet us at our progress.

"Ready?" Founder asked.

"Sure thing!" I chimed in while Honor rustled his mane. We trotted down a small, unpaved path that had likely been created by nothing but footsteps and were welcomed into the woods. I heard things all around me, but saw nothing.

"Today," Founder perked up, "I am going to introduce you to my family. As you said, most people see a park. I understand this is what the signs say. But for me, this is a house without walls. You feel the walls in your home and family, Will. But here, you will notice they have clearly been broken down. A house without walls is a powerful thing and I sense one day it will be just as powerful in your culture as it is here. Honor will help lead you into this meaning. I, for one, am excited to see that kind of life-giving wreckage, and in the suburbs no less." He smirked with an extra measure of coyness.

One of the sounds I'd been hearing was definitely getting louder, and much more frequent. My nerves were a little on edge, although Founder's presence, as well as riding so high upon Honor, certainly helped with that. I knew this place as a park, but there was no "park-feel" from where we stood. It was as wild as it gets. The rustling I had been hearing quickly turned into sight and my face must have gone white—white like the wolf I was now staring face-to-face in our path. He stood directly before us without moving a muscle. I wished he would run away, recognizing the towering horse and the eagle by my side. The other part of me wished I would run away, fearing the wolf lunging at me much like at the enclosure when Founder and I first met. But Honor was going nowhere, he was actually pointing directly for the wolf.

I looked up at Founder hoping for some direction. But Founder wasn't looking at me, he had both eyes locked on the wolf, and he was higher than I last noticed him. There was a different look in his eyes, one I hadn't seen before. His speed was increasing and the intensity of the eagle was more than evident. The wolf was about twenty yards away, and now, Founder was flying—almost diving—directly for him! Now I was afraid for Founder. I didn't want to lose him, especially while fighting on my behalf, but he, if anyone was wise to the wolf culture, understood and would never do anything rash. Honor kept walking forward—slowly—but without any reservation. Founder was still on a collision course with the wolf and couldn't be stopped now.

"Founder! Nooo!" I yelled.

Founder had become like family to me, perhaps that's why he was making such a statement. The wolf stood still, aware of Founder but still looking directly at us, when Founder threw on the breaks and eased in at the last second. At first I was relieved, but still didn't know what the wolf would do to him. "I'm who you want!" I jumped and yelled just as Founder landed on the wolf, but there was zero measure of attack. And at that very moment they both laughed hysterically and hit the ground with a roll. What a relief, they were friends.

"No!" Founder spoke up. "He is not my friend," referencing the wolf in response to my assumption. "Kainos is family."

"I'm sorry, what? You two, you're *family*? And what did you say his name was?"

"Will, you can speak directly with him, it's ok."

Honor walked towards him without fear, or the suspicion that I have to admit was still more than a little alive within me. "Kainos is your name? Forgive my struggle, it's just that, well, um, I haven't had many good experiences with wolves. And on a lesser note, I've never heard that name before."

"It means 'new'," Kainos said in a deep, worn, drawn-out voice. His fur looked old and brittle, with large tufts removed, mangled and obviously symbolic of a rugged life. "But it wasn't always the name I was known by, until, well—until others like Founder began to value me differently than I ever had previously experienced. Because of Founder and what he saw in me—unlike anyone else ever had—I was made new. New perspective won't only change your life, but also causes you to honor others differently."

Honor let out a muffled but resounding agreement before Kainos continued. "I am proof of this."

"I am sorry for acting, or assuming, that you were like any other wolf."

"Will," Founder interrupted, "You have no need to be afraid of the wolves, but you do need to be wise towards the wolf culture. Kainos is different, he is new."

Founder chuckled, and the others joined him.

"Kainos is my brother. Perhaps not by birth, but we are no less family. And that is how I will always see him. While I may have helped see and honor the good hidden within Kainos, he is who helped me learn the true meaning of family. In the animal kingdom that is what we are. The truest definition of kingdom is family. That is how we have learned to see one another, and that is the only way we have survived the attacks on our culture. Family has become our strength and has empowered us not only to survive, it's enabled us to thrive and flourish once again amid a culture of extinction. We need one another. When I speak of this culture of family, I am not talking about the institutional, legal form of family you may know of from your culture. I am talking about the culture of family that lives in a house without walls, a family that is love and life giving, honoring one another and even our differences in a way that, contrary to popular opinion, actually makes us stronger. I know you haven't seen a whole lot of this anymore where you come from, but we have survived and defeated the wolf culture by becoming family."

Without a moment of impasse, as Founder spoke that final sentence, I watched in awe as animal after animal flooded in to this narrow path in the woods.

Kainos stepped closer and began to speak softly, like a wise patriarch who had once been broken, now speaking with the strength of one much revived.

"I got my new name from this family. Founder saw it in me first, but it came alive through this tribe. We are many tribes come together, so much so that anymore we cannot see where one begins and the other ends. We are still very different, and hopefully that will never change. Honor led the way for all of us the way he is for you now. Without Honor, we would never have learned to use our perspective to value one another in the ways that have been most life giving to us each."

"When I was very young," Kainos continued, "I lost my family. Such is the case for many species here at Yellowstone—and beyond. I found myself without the foundation I so desperately wanted, and needed. I had one or two blood family members that survived, but they became so embittered and afraid that they lived only for themselves. They lost sight of how to value others because of the fear and insecurity they took on. I too became very bitter for a time. Like arthritis in my soul, I could feel my hope wasting away and the cavern of hurt breaking down and dividing my ability to truly love. I lived the wolf culture towards those like you, and towards those all around us here today."

"I preyed on others, and kept even more at a comfortable, fearful distance. Figuratively speaking, I wore sheep's clothing, convincing even myself at times that what I was doing was normal and even expected of a wolf such as me. My heart had grown cold and afraid, but I couldn't let that fear show. Little did I know that my fear shone through everything I did, it's just that most others, *like me*, were too blind to see it either. Most of the decisions I made in life were fear-based, with the motive of protecting myself. It made most things justifiable. The premise of the wolf culture only confirmed those justifications any time I needed to be convinced. In my heart, I wanted to be different. But I had fear on one side, hurt on another, and a culture around me that told me not to change—but to become more of a wolf."

Kainos paused as he shook his head, tears now streaming down his face. "I believed the lies from my culture because they hid how I really felt. They covered my wounds that I had to secretly lick and nurture every day as I tried to sleep. I was afraid to be different, afraid to expose my fears and pain to those who might dig their nails in them, or further embed the thorns in my paws rather than plucking them out. My culture of wolves tried to tell me who I was and who I wasn't; they removed choices for their so-called gentle reminder of what I needed to do, and they showed me a limited ceiling of expectations, until I realized they were stealing from within me. This continued up to the point when I met Founder. He had a different vision of me, and a different vision for me. It was hard to receive at first, but I had to keep fighting for that unseen truth that, deep down, I always wanted to believe. The light in Founder's eyes helped prove that the good part of me was indeed true. I'm a different kind of wolf now."

Founder's wings draped over Kainos with a brotherly love.

"Honor has been the key for all of us to tell you the truth," Founder stated with a generous nod towards their quiet companion. "Honor is the one who first introduced us. He saw us both for who we were in difficult times in our lives. Honor saw me at my worst, and still loved me enough to lead me forward. He didn't look at me for what had happened in my past life, Honor saw me for who I was. He has been the glue to our family here. Will, like Kainos, I too lost my family too early. I became a lone eagle, used to soaring high on my own; culturally independent in a way that was a great strength, and a weakness. I could dance with skies trying to forget the family I still needed, all the while Kainos had become a lone wolf. Independence is actually one of the biggest values and tactics of the wolf culture. It can sink its teeth into one, but can't get its mouth around a whole family. I wasn't able to use my true gift of vision without such a family around me. Honor helped me see that, and he helped me use my gift again as a purpose to empower others—such as Kainos himself. We would have never met, or gotten along, except for the way Honor led us. He didn't speak, as you have learned, but taught us to listen as he listened. Honor pointed at differences in our lives together that actually could become great compliments.

Such differences and quirks didn't necessarily need to be changed, but understood and appreciated. He showed us how to value and esteem those places in one another. We couldn't receive words from Honor, but he taught us how to give them on his behalf. He re-defined family for us."

Honor lowered his head, almost blushing, which was unusual to see from a horse of his quality. He remained quiet—mostly unnoticed—but never unfelt when around. His presence made everyone better and had obviously changed the culture they lived in. Honor appeared to seek little for self and yet hoisted up and carried so many others forward, together.

Founder, Kainos, and the others turned and began walking again. Honor led me closely behind, following their path. He couldn't speak to teach me, but I started to notice how much I was learning, just as Founder had predicted, simply through feeling Honor underneath me. His movements and ways, ever so slight, helped me to feel something other than insecurity. I wanted wings; the other dreams had made me crave such. But I was sure now that wings would be nothing if Honor wasn't the breeze I was mounted upon, just as he carried me forward now into this dream, Honor would likely lead me into all I hoped would come.

We twisted and turned, on the path and off. I got to know a number of fascinating members of this family as we walked. I looked around and from an outside view it certainly seemed an unusual group. But, there was something I could now start to point to within each one that seemed to tie them together, pointing to something greater than each individual creature. There was something living out of each of them, proving nothing was stagnant within. Kind of like the river and the pond. This family had something unusual about it that broke all the molds of family I once relied on. Their version of unique, unbridled togetherness reinvigorated the honor I often heard my parents request, but in a different sort of way. They demanded it, but now I saw it perhaps different even than what they were asking for. Family lines had been broken down in this animal kingdom, but they seemed to have been rebuilt in an even stronger way. Their definition of family gave me hope for what was possible!

I was enjoying the walk, learning from so many along the way. But our path had hit a dead end after an abrupt exit from the woods. Here before us stood a high piled mountain of giant rocky boulders with a cave at its foundation, hoisting up pine trees in every possible crevice. Slowly, but apparently right on cue, a large bear began to throw its weight side-to-side and waddle towards us out of its slumber. Founder hopped up next to it and began to whisper in the bear's ear. They exchanged these whispers back and forth with a nod here and there until Founder once again hopped back over beside me. Honor knelt to the ground, obviously directing me that it was time to dismount. I tentatively climbed off of this generous horse and felt like I was standing on my legs for the very first time again. If I had tried to walk I'd probably have waddled like the bear, perhaps not as gracefully though. "Do you feel new?" The bear asked me in an almost motherly tone.

"Uhh, yeah, I suppose I do—in a whole bunch of ways though. What should I be feeling? Other than this imprint Honor has left on me, that is," I quipped.

The bear bypassed my question and began to share what sounded like a bedtime story that I should sit down for. Founder leaned over and whispered in my ear, not wanting to interrupt. "This is Mama Bear. Just listen," he said softly, and faced forward again so as to be clearly attentive to her story. Her voice was a treasure with its deep, sweet, southern drawl that seemed foreign for these parts.

"I was often averse to what, and especially *whom* was new. I wanted little to do with change. I had my patterns of life and was set in my ways. I was an only mom with one cherished cub. His name was Promise. I did all I could to give him the best life of a bear, living the fat side of the wild. I was overly protective, I now know that looking back, but it was only because I was trying to guard Promise from anything or anyone that might harm him, he was such an innocent creature. We went about our routines; we played, gathered, ate, and slept. Life was good! But not like it could have been. I had my own ways all drawn out about what a family and a bear life should look like, and I was stubborn as all get out, I mean, I am his mama and all. You see, back then, that's when it started to change for me—when I became new. Way back then, I was a mama bear. But today, I stand before you as Mama Bear. I know it doesn't sound like much, but there's a big, fat difference that I learned the hard way."

No one breathed a word, or made a sound. Everyone sat so still, respectfully in awe of the story that Mama Bear was sharing, as if they too were listening for the very first time. I felt like I was in another world. And truly, I was. As weird as it seemed, I didn't feel like I was dreaming anymore, I just felt so at home, even right in front of the cave. As childish as it felt, I loved sitting here listening to this bear talk, like something I would have read about or watched in a movie. There was something authentic—almost soothing—and it resonated with my soul. I could listen to her tell stories all day long.

"Have you heard of the word *adoption* in your culture little man?"

If I wasn't so captivated I may have been slightly put off by the "little man" reference. And not wanting to deter her by making some dumb comment in an attempt at a joke, I simply nodded in agreement. "Well, good! But, and that's a big fat butt," she laughed at herself wildly, wiggling her big bottom in the dirt in a confident sort of way, all too proud of herself. "Adoption doesn't completely mean what you probably think it means," she said with a wise prickly tone. "Adoption doesn't just mean a child is legally part of your family, it's mmuuuuuucchhhhh bigger than that, and it's not just kids either. Nope, nuh, uh! Adoption can happen on a much bigger level, just look at what you've learned already about all these fine creatures. They're family. We're family. And I almost missed out on my place in such a family being all stuck in my own ways and perspectives and all. But there were others just waiting to be loved, and to love me. Promise taught me that, God rest his soul."

My heart broke at her words, just realizing what she had said, about Promise. She obviously loved being a mama; I can't imagine how much it must have hurt. "It did hurt," she bristled, "still does. But Promise taught me a bigger meaning of family that was waiting for me. While I tried to hold onto him and me, and make our cave and life enough, he was out doing what I should have been. I may have lost my cub, but I still have even more of Promise through this family right here."

"See, I was trying to keep Promise from spreading his wings, and us from losing our family. I was a protective mama. We were all each other had. But Promise, he wasn't trying to protect our family; he knew that would stay intact as long as our hearts did. He was out trying to grow our family. He kept bringing one new friend after another, different species of creatures, young and old, back to our cave. I would get all nervous nelly and let out a roar to scare them away from Promise, and from our family home. He took what we had and gave it away freely like I would to him. The way I saw him as family, that's how he saw everyone else. He was but a cub who was adopting the world!"

Honor interrupted with a loud, roaring sound of agreement.

"Yes, that's right Honor, you tell 'em. Honor and Promise became best pals and started meeting everyone together. People outright changed when encountering those two."

"If Honor was our glue," Founder spoke strongly, "then Promise helped us see a little bit of himself that was hidden away in us all, and in everyone else too. He brought out parts of us that we had locked away to protect from the culture of wolves we fought for so many years. Honor held us together, but Promise, he was what we all started to see in one another."

Mama Bear began to cry, having a hard time composing herself now. And who could blame her?

"We all did become family, didn't we?"

Everyone nodded together, firmly in agreement.

"And we'll just keep on growing, looking for those who need to be strengthened with us, no matter how different. Promise was great at that." She finished while wiping away a tear.

"Founder," she began to ask tears now rolling down

her face. "Will you finish the story for me, dear?"

"Of course, Mama, I'd be honored. See, Will, Promise always saw the potential in everyone, and Honor always helped him draw it out. But one day, Promise came across a young sheep friend. Promise saw some of himself in that little sheep and began pursuing him. He was determined to love him until the sheep knew what love was. And he really was a sheep; there was no disguise at all. However, that little sheep was led with the others right back into the dens—well, back then they were dens. He didn't know any better, and he truly appreciated what Promise was trying to bring about in his life, but he couldn't resist following, perhaps fearing what Promise was telling him wouldn't be true. Mama was trying to protect Promise from getting hurt, and warned him in all sorts of ways. But he was so accustomed to Mama always speaking against such unfettered love that Promise didn't recognize the true warning that was there this time. Will, Promise went into the den one day after that sheep and never came out. Bear and all, the wolves never allowed him to see what might become of his powerful bear cub life. But, Will, we still see that power every day. If anything, it hasn't slowed us down from living a culture built around family or adopting so many creatures as our own, it's only strengthened it. Promise's life taught us a new way to live. So when he died, Promise multiplied *through us*. That, Will, is how we became a true family."

"I've got it from here, Founder. Thank you, dear. I

miss my boy!" She spoke again to us all, though clearly looking at me. "That will never change. But if I had lived more like him, and learned a new way, I might have been able to get him to listen to some of my wisdom as well when there was true danger at hand. Yep, I've got my regrets, many of 'em. But I don't regret Promise living the way he did. He inspired me to let the Promise live from within me towards others. His example has made our lives and culture so rich, I don't even care what my cave is like anymore. Promise broke down all our walls and re-modeled our lives and family as he gave his little life for others to know the kind of love and family that he knew. His life, gave us all family. And hopefully, many more will learn from his redemptive tale in the times to come."

And with that, Mama Bear slowly made her way back into her cave. "Family," Founder rose up in speech, "is the one culture that can spread in a world changing way. But, it must be reinterpreted from its typical limits and categories. In your culture, there are many homes and families with walls not just around them; those lines are actually in between them. Instead of growing and multiplying further, they're getting thinner. Family has become a weakness of your culture when it once was a great strength. It can become strong—even stronger— once again, Will, but you must break down those outer walls for the divisions inside to fall as well. The definition of family will become one with the nature of adoption, not always literally, but in how you live and give love to those around you, and honor who is hidden inside each person that you meet. There is great promise in family, as you heard today. But that promise will not be realized until you learn to honor again, both those within your family, and to honor the value in those currently outside your walls. Only then will the walls begin to fall down and family be revived once again. Too many of creation's own are hurting in this world, those who have lost family members to death or disagreement, and even those who've never had a family. Some of those disagreements will be repaired, but love will become a new agreement that releases the promise resting within every life and home. Will, Mama Bear is right. Promise still lives in this family. He can live in yours too!"

****

That dream left me wanting more, but not the same kind of more I'd already been so keen for. It helped me see the many new, possible definitions of life and family already at hand. I didn't know where to begin. And I couldn't, yet. Because when I awoke from that dream it was still the middle of the night, with several hours left to sleep. I took a deep breath, and with a smile on my face, perhaps more comfortable than I'd been in years, leapt joyfully back into sleep.

Chapter 12:
The Eighth Dream:
Four Corners

"They who can give up essential liberty to obtain a little temporary safety deserve neither liberty or safety."

- Benjamin Franklin

I could taste and feel the gritty sand in my teeth. I was panting like a dog and felt like I was waking up from a bad dream, but I wasn't in my bed. I think I was in the desert. But I couldn't tell where for sure.

What I did know is that I felt as thirsty as I had ever been—and besides figuring out where I was, my number one goal was simply to find some water to drink. The cottonmouth was almost gagging in itself, and my skin bristled from the sand kicking up in quick gusts of wind all around me, pelting me like I was in the middle of a giant Airsoft war. How I wished I really had been. That would be fun. Wherever I was, it was confusing, and to top things off my eyesight was now blurry and of no help at all. Besides that, the heat was sweltering. From all appearances it was the middle of the day and the sun was now beating down on me—hard. Unsure of what else to do, I began walking. I didn't think I could get much more lost already having no clue where I was. At home, having a sense of direction is easy, just look for the mountains and that's west. Here, not so much.

A large windstorm whipped in before I could duck for cover. It blasted me, especially my eyes. They began watering profusely, and everything became that much more blurry—not to mention painful! I had never experienced anything like this before, and my thirst was only growing. I needed help. But before I could even finish that thought I felt large talons come down and grip my shoulders.

"Founder," I sighed with relief. "I can't see. Can you help me?"

"Of course," he responded quickly, "but I can't stay here. I can't survive in the desert but I will point you in the right way."

I felt his grip get a little tighter, and nudge me until I finished turning my body's positioning towards his guidance.

"Go this way, and I will see you soon. Start walking and your sight will return soon enough."

He released my shoulders and disappeared quickly.

Either way, I was thankful. My eyes were still killing me, but the blur was going away. I kept my focus on the ground, my closest and easiest point of sight for the time being, plus, it shielded my eyes from the sand still whipping in the air. Cautiously, like walking in a pitch-black room, I moved forward.

"Ouch!" I yelled—almost mid-thought—feeling the tiny but merciless pokes of the cactus sinking into my skin, and the top of my head now feeling like it'd been prepared for porcupine duty. I guess I couldn't see the unpleasant plant very well while staring at my feet. I resolved myself to start looking up again, but still couldn't decipher much of the terrain. I think I had slightly veered my path from the course Founder set me in to meet such a prickly friend already, but I didn't know what else to do except to keep making my way forward, as straight as I could.

After another hundred or so paces, my eyes started to open a little more clearly. At this point, I was outright panting. The desert was having its way with my eyes and my insides felt like they were drying up quickly. I could, however, see something of substance up in the distance.

So, I kept striding towards it, but a little more carefully this time. No need to make friends with another cactus. The sun was brighter than I had ever had the privilege of—very draining—but I was thankful that my eyes were steadily improving. My goal was simple; find water at the structure ahead. From the looks of it I was getting close.

Weakness and thirst were tag-teaming me. But the nearing proximity of the structure ahead seemed to help my hope and strength to rise just enough. I picked up my pace. Was this what I thought it was, an answer to my prayers? Liquid love was waiting. Water! A towering mountain overflowing with waterfall-like streams and what was some sort of cycling mote all around it—like a river, but going in circles. No wonder Founder directed me this way; it was the same kind of refuge Founder himself had become to my own dryness of life and home. I picked up my pace until hitting a slightly tentative jog— anxious but not wanting to meet yet another surprise in my path, though my eyes seemed to be doing much better. I was feeling woozy more than anything.

My thirst was heightened by its own hope, but it didn't matter at this point compared to the answer set before me. I ran directly towards the river-like mote that encompassed the mountain and leapt from the ground to jump in. I could already feel the satisfaction baptizing my scaly, sand beaten body, believing it would be a bit of a balm for my eyes as well. I took a deep breath pre-leap that only paved the way for what became a painful, crashing thud. I belly flopped like a caught fish tossed to the deck. My split lip could vouch for the hard, dry sand—cement like. Frustrated tears flooded down my face, which probably seemed like a torrential downpour compared with what *this* place was used to. Apparently that was the only moisture this ground had known in some time. This "paradise" I went for was nothing but a mirage—a cold-hearted, hopeless mirage.

I lied motionless for some time, not just losing hope, but now I even found myself waist deep in anger, something I hadn't felt since these dreams grabbed hold of my life. I'd experienced it all too frequently before my introduction to Founder, and memories of such were popping up again like unwanted weeds, which only stood to inflict more damage if I allowed them residence. How could I have believed? What happened? I could barely even finish a thought. The emptiness of this wasteland was drying me up inside, which impaired my sight far more than any blast of sand could. I was confused, and felt more lost. But, Founder? I began to remember. He...I...I don't understand. At that very moment I heard a noise, and it felt like something arrived suddenly on the scene. I felt his talons again. If relief had a voice, it was mine.

"Founder!" I screamed, as I flipped over, now with enough hope to forget the beating I'd taken. But when I looked in his eyes every bit of that joy became as parched as my thirst.

"Oh, I'm not Founder, my boy. But I did lead you this way."

I was scrambling in my thoughts, putting together pieces that just wouldn't fit. I didn't understand. But, he, I mean, you…

"Oh, you may have assumed I was Founder, and I suppose I took advantage of your trust, just a bit," this nasty vulture spoke so crassly, yet with pleasure. I could feel the slime oozing out of him, but I was already a bit too far into his world.

"What are you doing to me?" I asked fearfully.

"No worries mate, I'm not going to do anything to you. In a place like this, you will do what I seek to yourself. I'll just wait patiently and prey on what the elements life—or lack thereof—bring my way."

He screeched off with a caw that cackled so loud and awful I could hear it echo inside me as if on repeat. The sound ignited fears in me that had been falling away only a dream ago. I watched him join his friends circling high and quiet above—obviously assuming there would be life to prey on even before there was any death to see. These vultures didn't just wait for death as I'd often been told; they devoured the last bits of the lives that were wasting away in the desert, those led by the mirage of desperate desires. Reminded me of the wolves, perhaps an accomplice. I battled with my mind for a way out. I was starving for sight, not of my eyes, but of the nourishing vision that came from within. I couldn't find any though. I had to keep breathing hope until the vultures and their lies had none. I was deserted here, except for those last few drops I was trying to muster up from within.

I got up and walked where the mirage once stood, or at least where I had concocted it in my mind, looking for any kind of clue to help me navigate. I walked slowly, and curiously, still stung, but searching everywhere for a glimmer of something that clearly didn't exist. I must have just finished walking through what I'd thought was the mountain spring. This had to be where it ended. But that's when it hit me, or actually, when I hit it. It was the suddenness that was most jarring, "Ouch!" I yelled, slamming into what looked like nothing, but the object's strength had something else to say on the subject.

"What was that?" I asked aloud while rubbing my forehead, hadn't my head already taken enough? I thought so. It felt like an all too solid wall, yet, there was nothing to be seen anywhere. I tried reaching my arm in several different directions, but that only had me searching, like an evasive sleeve too early on a dark morning. Something was really wrong. I could see now for miles ahead. But I couldn't manage to get past this invisible blockade. How hard had my head hit that wall anyway? But this was no mirage anymore. In fact, it seemed to be quite the opposite.

I kept walking, feeling my way over to the right of

where the wall and I had collided. "Ouch!" I yelled aloud once more, slamming my shoulder while it too jumped in on this game of discovery. I started to move my hands up and down the invisible limits and realized I was staring into what could only be a hidden corner. It was terribly confusing, and to be honest, a little frightening. According to my new discoveries, space seemed to be shrinking, making me claustrophobic. I looked up and saw the vultures still above me, almost smirking and flaunting their empty stomachs. They weren't circling anymore, but were perched on top of, well, on top of what sight would show as nothing. But, that wasn't entirely possible either. They were obviously sitting on whatever structure made up this corner because they were perfectly still, suspended in mid air. They were indeed very high up, but watched me closely from the top of whatever these invisible bounds were, no doubt a more friendly home to them than to me.

The toll the dryness was taking on me was rising quickly. I did my best to ignore it and put my hands back on the wall in front of me, I moved gingerly back to the left in the direction I had come from. Step by step I followed my hands along the surface of this great wall of nothing. With every step I glanced again, still trying to look through this solid, glasslike hindrance; wanting to move forward freely into what was on the other side, remaining kept by what I could not see. It was a paradox for sure. I had no answers. Founder was still nowhere to be seen. I was breathing so heavily now that I was losing focus, back to a place of simply surviving. The battle was surely between my sinking thoughts, and my will. I couldn't allow worry to apprehend what I was learning about unseen truths, each one seemed to naturally gravitate towards the lies instead.

As I made my way down the wall I again saw another large, misplaced building in the distance—full of light! In fact, it looked like a lighthouse from where I stood, but I was also the same person who thought my last destination was a water-encompassed haven. So, I wasn't exactly getting my hopes up. More than anything, I realized I needed to focus on keeping my peace, because then, no matter what I came across, good or bad, it couldn't dictate my vision. I couldn't give that away anymore, especially to mere circumstances. Speaking of which, I couldn't see the vultures anymore which led me to believe—and perhaps naively so—that they were but a distant memory. Wishful thinking, or maybe I was actually turning into an optimist after all this time being around Founder. Ha, that would give Mom a laugh for sure. Either way, I assumed they couldn't touch me without permission. The vultures surely followed the breadcrumbs of the wolves to their table; I simply had to live counter to such culture. Easier said than done I suppose, but I had to persevere with a different kind of hope, one that couldn't be stolen by mere pressure or circumstance. My hope had to be attached to something bigger, even if unseen. No wonder they call them dreams.

Using one hand after the other, I scaled the wall sideways. My feet were on the ground, but my eyes focused ahead, zeroing in on the lights and their schizophrenic patterns. Whatever they were, leery as I might be, they were compelling.

The lights were flashing now, brighter and brighter, with a multitude of colors. That's when I realized what I was walking on, *red carpet.* Incredibly odd, but little else fit in either. From all I'd been learning though, I realized that I grew up herded into believing a lot of odd things I never took time to question. So why should this be any different? Perhaps, now, deceptions were simply being exposed for what they really were. It was as velvety as an awards show, and its path actually relieved a little navigational pressure. I had been so determined to move forward along the supposed wall that I really hadn't paid attention to what was under my feet—until now—with no idea where or when it began.

It was a beautiful, soft material that, like the majority of things here, was extremely out of place upon the grainy sand it lied on. I plucked by hands from the wall and let the carpet take over instead. Even that renewed my freedom a bit. It was exhausting trying to stay on an invisible wall, as if scaling a small rock ledge far too high up. The vivid path allowed me to breathe freely again while I walked, rather than suspiciously placing one hand after the other in investigative fashion. The lights grew brighter with every bounce of freedom, and I felt a lot stronger just being upon the carpet. It was invigorating actually. My previous thirst seemed to wane and the lights might as well have been a multitude of cameras flashing in my direction. It was liberating, powerful, and I have to admit, a hypnotizing sort of fun. Shaking off all the exhaustion like I'd been buried in the sand instead of walking upon it, I felt set free by the brightness before my eyes and the bounce under my feet. Hope itself was flashing *at* me now.

"Welcome to The New You!"

The sign flashed in lights, capturing my attention and arresting the memory of many such thoughts I remembered having often in the privacy of my own room. Founder had shown me something like this, but far different. It didn't take long to remember that I had to separate the truth from the lies, and that this wasn't what I was here for, let alone the dream I wanted. Nevertheless, I was still slightly curious. I felt so much more in control hitting that red carpet, without the burdens I'd felt before. I was pretty sure I could handle it and just know when to say when.

There had been so many occasions when I wanted a new me. So many times when I looked at those around me jealously. Too many times when I felt the weight of my circumstances and wished for something else. There were a lot of seasons in my life, even the season I was in before meeting Founder, which had me looking for hope by re-inventing myself. What if I was taller, more successful, more loved, stronger, faster, smarter, thinner, more powerful, or if my family and I had more wealth? What if we were famous or popular? What if? What if? What if? It was an intriguing question for sure, one that I wrestled with less now, especially after the cave of mirrors. But here it was before me again, written in bright lights—"Welcome to the New You!" I stepped up to the door, flung it open and walked in—and the red carpet subtly slithered away.

This too was a house of mirrors in all directions, but far different than what I experienced hidden in Mt. Rushmore, one like you might see at a carnival but far more luxurious. Different mirrors, one after another lined the walls, each framed differently, some wider and some taller, some lit up with a spotlight and others dimmed in a corner. They were all unique, so I decided to browse a little.

The first mirror was unusually tall. It offered a perfect portrayal of myself that I'd never seen before. I liked what I saw! My presence was towering and strong, it made me feel a superiority I had always longed for—too often feeling just the opposite in my life. This was a welcome change, a sense of redemption. I stood in front of that mirror and most everything else seemed to melt away. I straightened my shirt, and my posture. I faced forward, lifted my chin and smiled.

Wow! This is the kind of mirror I'd like to have. As much as I wanted to just keep staring, my curiosity got the better of me like a hook, dragging me towards the other mirrors.

The next mirror was a halting reality. It called the last reflection an utter liar, and in fact, I looked worse than I ever thought I had. My skin looked grayish, dull and altogether lacking life. My posture was off-kilter, I was slightly misshapen if I dare to say so, and I never knew my nose was so awkwardly large. What's worse, this mirror reflected against the previous one, a nasty comparison I could do without, leaving me stuck and confused between the two. One aroused self-confidence, the other drilled me further down, but they were even worse together, feeling like I might as well be right back in the wasteland of the vulture's desert. I jumped to the next mirror.

This one was again completely different. This mirror reflected a light from the distance that made it look like it was shining out of me. I had a glow like a movie star might carry, and could only imagine what others would have thought had they been here to see. I almost started to believe the light when I remembered the previous mirror, the one that even new clothes couldn't perfect. It hit me like a hard slap and jarred me from what I wanted to believe. Ugh! It felt like a game, like the world was having its way with me—high, low, high, low. Whatever! I tried to shake it off but it was more like slime this time, a heavy condemnation based slime trying to lure me deeper still, and so far it was winning. I think it only took me up so I would fall even harder, further, when I inevitably crashed.

My knees started to buckle and weaken. The bounce I found on the red carpet disappeared in those mirrors, and apparently was never all that real in the first place. I figured such was the case, but it's amazing how quickly we can get trapped back into facades we should recognize without desire to re-enter. There it went, false freedom—again—and a lying strength. I knew better, and had even cautioned myself of this going in. My view of self was up and down from mirror to mirror, and I couldn't seem to escape it anywhere I looked, constantly being redirected and influenced, one reaction to another. I turned left and then spun back around again. I looked forward, and then up towards the mirror on the ceiling. All the reflections were confusing and lied about the one before, or perhaps each one was simply lying on its own. Which one do I really measure up to? Which one is true? One puffed me up, and the other threw me down, a day in professional wrestling is what it might as well have been. But in all reality, even my dreams reminded me that I'd had plenty of days like this in the real world too, days that felt like a world full of paparazzi teasing me with gossip about myself—good and bad—probably just playing games with me.

My mind ran rampant. Who am I? How do I want others to see me? What do others already think of me? Do they see me like that first mirror, or like the second?

I quivered looking back in thought. The more I measured myself, whether against others or the world, I lost every time. Even if against my own perception of me, it didn't matter. The bottom line was the more I looked at myself, the weaker I became. I had created my own quicksand apparently, and it was worse than the desert outside! These mirrors themselves were alive and measuring me like tailors with the wrong sort of tux, and I had been tricked into offering them my reflection for their fodder.

But all I wanted was what Founder saw. It was the only thing that had ever made me feel genuinely good—*from the inside out.* I longed for the Cave of Mirrors that left me a horizon of possibility, where wings were easily spread, rather than to be defined by anything like this. I thought of Founder and his mom at the zoo. The passers by were his mirrors. His mom was the blind one, yet could truly see. I knew which one I wanted to be. I knew which one Founder was teaching me to be. And neither had anything to do with creating a new me, just seeing myself correctly.

I knew what I had to do. With all my strength of mind I took my glare and focus off of the mirrors so they couldn't glare back. I closed my eyes and remembered what the light had shown me before. Looking from within me I walked forward slowly but determined with eyes closed and my hands out before me. I thought I had seen a door at the end of the hallway. I remembered back to Founder's words, "If you can't see in the dark, you can't see at all." To walk blindly was my only chance to get there without sinking into self again. That would be my goal.

I stammered and fell a couple times, but it was all worth it not to gaze into the lies that didn't seem to stop watching me, each of which was quite adept at selling itself for my attention. I never went in looking for an answer, and still found myself bludgeoned by the perspectives of the wolves. As I walked, it felt like I had been beaten head-to-toe by such measurements and opposing reflections. But perhaps the bruising was really only felt in my mind, because there was no one else around and I'd seen enough versions of self to classify a gang.

My hand hit what had to be a door and I snapped open my eyes, only to find a mirror staring back within it. I put my eyes permanently on the doorknob and flung the door as hard as I ever had, sure to pass each and every insecurity, and I leapt out—landing on my feet and unwilling to look back. But it didn't take long to realize I was before yet another invisible wall.

"What is this place?" I cried. "Somebody, help!" I yelled even louder.

I put both hands up against the glass that again I could not see, but a limit I continued to feel, and leaned in tired and dejected. My face was pressed up against the glass without restraint when I opened one eye, sighing loudly in exhaustion.

And there he was! It was Founder. He was on the other side of the wall now, but I couldn't hear a thing. I didn't think that was as big a deal for him, as he probably knew exactly what I was up against, as well as my every thought. I wished I could hear him. I needed the help, and the direction. Then I realized something. He told me that I should know his voice, and after all our time together thus far I realized that perhaps I did know it better than I thought, it was ingrained deep within me but only drawn out when I was the one to throw it the buoy. I could listen deeply and at the very least watch and follow him as he moved. There was only one way to do this of course, and that was along the unseen path of the wall, away from the wiles of the wilderness, and keeping vision for the other side.

I followed Founder side-by-side and simply wished—as I had many times now—that I could fly, more specifically that I could fly up over the imposing wall. I'd shoot right up over this wall and join him with a barrel roll in the air. But maybe that was still for another dream, and there was no use focusing on what I couldn't do; I'd done enough of that already. Now, I needed to follow Founder like his shadow. I was the shadow on the other side of the freedom I needed, and re-connecting with him in such a united way was clearly my only way forward.

To be truthful, it was frustrating to follow him like

this, like hope was a breath away but impossible to get to. With our destination still unknown I was thankful not to be alone anymore. He brought something out in me that I was only beginning to learn how to bring out of myself, which was all the more of a reminder to keep changing, learning to see in new ways—*no matter how uncomfortable it could be*. As the river had taught me, it's harder for the wolves to prey on fresh water.

We journeyed a ways up the wall before Founder stopped, urging towards me in a dramatic, new manner. He was giving me specific instructions of some sort, but I couldn't hear him and had a hard time understanding the game of charades he was forced to play with his wings. I couldn't help but laugh and even he noticed the failings of our communication. The way I had to connect with him now was just to look directly into his communicative eyes, which always seemed to tell the whole story, even if I could only read in part. The story we would live out however was still up to my translation and that's where it got a little sketchy.

I was so nervous to the do the wrong thing, or misunderstand, that at first I found myself doing the exact opposite of Founder. He'd lift up his right wing, and I would jump the other direction. He'd lift his left wing and I pounced even further the wrong way. It probably looked like a bad game of Simon Says. I just needed to relax. My dehydration was growing strong again, likely just more noticeable, but far past the point of thirst. I was desperate.

I hoped, perhaps assumed, that he was leading me towards water, but truth be told I really had no way of knowing. Founder intended some very specific directions for me, of which I could make out little, except for the fact that he kept pausing to show me a clear, deep breath, adamantly urging me to try the same. He practiced this with me time and again, but I gathered nothing. It became quite boring. Obviously I had no clue why, and though it seemed out of place I was trying to embed such deep pause in my memory for when I might need it most; Founder always had a reason. And that's when I heard it....

Gonnngggggggg! Gonnngggggggg! Gonnngggggggg!

The loud, obnoxious sound continued steadily. It actually shook the very ground we stood on, and it was the first time I could see a glimmer of the invisible walls. Their vibrations gave them away as the light shuddered off the rattling glare, but only slightly.

Otherwise, I didn't see anything but open space in every direction, leaving me with absolutely no idea where it might be coming from. I peeled off from the wall as I saw Founder flying forward alongside it, as if to meet me later. He kept looking back, like a father dropping off his child at school for the first time. But he didn't appear worried. I couldn't figure out if that was a compliment, or a mistake, I laughed, knowing myself all too well.

I sped up suddenly, like the ringing sound of the clock automatically put some skip in my step, and a little extra focus too, which was probably a good thing. I felt a different pace already. But the further I walked the more I heard the sound evolve. Not only that, but it was coming from *every* direction.

Tick, tick, tick...

Gonnngggggggg, gonnngggggggg, gonnngggggggg.

The sounds were varied and definitely not connected, randomly bursting like geysers from the ground—from all sides. I still couldn't see where they might be coming from. I stopped to sit still and listen. Then I took another step. When I did I heard a new set of noises coming from another clock, this time like a beeping alarm. So I stopped again. I felt like I was back in the suburbs playing tag with our smoke detectors. Yeah, you could say I had knocked my fair share off the ceiling trying to discover which one dared provoke me with its incessant chirping. This was worse, and I was on the hunt. What's more is I now felt even more pressure to get out of this place, like time was literally ticking away. I stepped once more and heard another clock chime in. What is going on? I was incredulous. It didn't make any sense. There was no house, no clock tower, and nothing electronic in sight—only sounds.

"Grrrr, *shut up*!" I yelled impatiently. "Enough!"

I sped up my pace, itching to figure out what was happening. As the noise got louder, I got nuttier. That smoke detector game was taking on a whole new meaning now, and it sounded like I'd need something bigger than a broomstick. But I didn't know what I was looking for anyway. That wouldn't stop me though. Time still felt like it was running out and I had to find the source. There were no people, no place, no animals—*nothing*. And at this point I could tell I was making the noises even worse within me. The ticking was becoming incessant in my mind, an elaborate scheme surely set up by my worst enemy, I had reasoned. There must have been at least twenty different clocks at the source of this combined racket. What was it trying to tell me? What was I missing? The noise of the ticking, chirping, alarming clocks was becoming so maddening it felt like time itself was trying to possess me.

"Aahhhhhhh," I cried out, totally stressed now and almost ready to give up—almost. It was taking me as its prisoner. But that's when I think I finally heard Founder's voice inside me. He must have been speaking awfully loud to compete with the clocks. I looked back on what he had been trying to instill in me before, with all that flapping. I stopped, and took a deep breath. Then I took another. Then another. Before I knew it, I couldn't even hear the clocks anymore, and time wasn't chasing me like I was chasing my own tail. I took another deep breath in, then out.

Everything became suddenly clear. The time had no control over me, nor the noises that it was trying to intimidate me with. With each deep breath, I could actually see through the noise. The clamor had me searching for something that did not exist, and actually began to lord itself over me. That quickly, I was bound by time rather than using it for my own purposes. I could see Founder now and he was directly ahead, but I could hear him teaching me inside as the professor of perspective that he is. He had turned what I now assumed to be the corner of the wall we walked down together and hovered at my height, staring at me intently from there. That's when it hit me. He had told me this long ago; *true dreams aren't bound by time.*

I arrived at the wall near Founder. He was smiling in his own beaked sort of smile. I walked alongside him for a bit and then I realized something. We were walking along another wall. This was the fourth wall, and the third corner I had found.

"It's a box," I cried out. "A box!"

I finally figured it out. This wilderness was in a big glass box, and Founder was in the real dream just outside of such. It was a dream inside a dream, though I personally would tend to say this box is more of a nightmare—but I'd learned all too well, all too often in my life it's what many others still refer to as a dream, I was just now realizing it was a bad one. I was ready to leave, but have to admit, I was still a bit curious as to what was in the fourth corner. I picked up my pace and began jogging along the wall, with Founder still faithfully at my side, the tip of his wing to my shoulder. I jogged for quite awhile, silently communicating with Founder the best I could until I saw it—what had to be the fourth corner of the box and the ultimate lure of such a wasted dream. It was a house, large and creatively built. But it was made out of stacks of money.

I didn't even want to think about going inside, not after everything else I had been through. I turned back towards Founder, looked deep inside and realized that all I had to do to escape this nightmare was to choose to wake up. Then, maybe hope would have the chance to breathe again. I sure needed to.

****

Looking back, many of the lessons from within that box were similar to what Founder had taught me in different forms throughout previous dreams. But, there was something to feeling their apparent reality for myself, and experiencing the counterfeit version of many of such. There was relief. Not just from waking up, but from having passed through those deceptions to breathe freely on the other side. What stirred me the most was the box. It was invisible, but present the whole time. It let me see as far through it as I wished, but never let me taste those supposed endless limits. It was the perfect deception, and it would have kept me going in circles, well, perhaps in squares, had I not been learning to believe for something more. It would be easy, every now and again, to find yourself back in the middle of its wilderness, leaving each corner with nothing but appeal. Who doesn't like to escape their life temporarily? I wouldn't have known to ask it back then, but sure makes me wonder why we'd ever need such escapes if we were truly living the dream?

Chapter 13:
The Ninth Dream: Downtown

"Nowadays people know the price of everything and the value of nothing." - Oscar Wilde

I was sitting on a bus bench next to a busy road, and Founder sat tall and proud with his chest puffed out to my side. There were people all around us, passers-by who, as a group, were very diverse. But, I don't think they could see us. It seems it would have been obvious if they could, a large bald eagle sitting next to me. I suppose I could have played him off as a large stuffed animal, as if I'd just come from an amusement park, but Founder had much too much life in him to pass for something so trivial.

"I might have thought we were awaiting a bus

marked, 'Wilderness'," Founder quipped back.

But I had come to know that any bus we would be riding on was much more likely to read, "Hope." I'd heard promises of such in politics for long enough, but now I knew that I already held the keys to what had gone unfulfilled. Truly, I didn't actually know if we were waiting for a bus of any kind. Founder didn't strike me as someone overly excited by automobiles, which were likely a bit of an inhibitor to his wings.

"Now, a convertible on the other hand…"

"That's a different kind of dream," Founder interrupted, still laughing. I liked the friendship we were building. It was nice to relate with him in such a relaxed fashion, especially since most of our adventures weren't what most would deem chill. No complaints here, though. My house was chill enough, and then some. Speaking of which, a sharp, cold wind knifed through us quickly, making me shiver. But such was the nature of standing in the shadows—especially downtown.

There were tall buildings standing up before us, and the life painted around the cluster of buildings was presenting itself in a variety of ways, people artistically painted across the streets with the diversity, and vibrancy, of the surrounding graffiti and murals. Compared to where I lived, life was spilling out over every curb here in all different forms and fashions. Poor, rich, students, business focused, homeless, the world's stamps were everywhere. I kind of enjoyed not being seen, it gave me a different perspective than usual. Typically, I might walk down the street and watch others, but would still have a self-awareness about me that probably kept me from seeing too freely, always half viewing life through my own self-consciousness; I was only now learning how much such a filter truly robbed, might as well have been a name for one of the wolves. What I was taking in felt different simply because we couldn't be seen, which allowed me to see without my standard double vision, blurring everything through my insecurity. But now, I was seeing sharper and clearer than ever, like the crispness of a new day. Founder was watching as well, but to be honest, he seemed much more focused on watching me. He turned to me with an eyebrow raised and half a smile, pondering our next move and knowing all too well what I was thinking—one of his many quirks.

"Will, don't look at the outer stamps the world is showing you, haven't we talked about this enough?" He spoke strongly, but graciously applied such a rebuke to me with gentle jest.

"Look past those. If you truly want to see a person, the outside visual may be what your eyes see first, but it's only an invitation into something much greater that may be hidden, hurting; or they may even have a happiness inside them that is looking to reach out to someone like you. Life looks different down here, but it really isn't. It is just more open. You can see what gets covered up where you live. Where you are there are more walls. Down here, there are more windows. But in the dream I am teaching you, there are big open doors."

I nodded in agreement, still wanting more of that dream he spoke of. I mean, I had heard all he'd been teaching me, but being with Founder still left me with a hunger I couldn't yet put into words. I could think of many times in life when I wanted something more, but there were only a handful of those that left me believing that more was actually possible, or within my grasp. As much as anything, that's what Founder conveyed. I found myself for once believing in my own ability to be a reformer of hope, instead of just one of the crowd holding on to its picturesque memory, wanting for what was or what could be. I wasn't a buyer or a seller, a glass half full or half empty, I was, in fact, one of hope's own recruits; self enlisted into an array of lights that together create hope's form, especially on top of the darkest of backdrops.

Life was spinning on a different axis in those moments and I didn't want it to tilt back the other way—truly afraid that without him, it might. I loved spending time with Founder for this very reason; he became a foundation not for anchors sake but for life's true launch. I mean, I enjoyed the lessons, gobbled them up actually, and I loved his frien…family that is, but there was something to be said for just walking near to him. He bred something in me that both healed and inspired at the same time. I wanted to look at life that way. I wanted to spread my wings wide, but it wasn't just a desire for more freedom. Everyone wants that it seems, though from everything I've watched it seems the more we chase it, the less we have. But it wasn't something to be captured as much as it is to be lived.

It wasn't just more freedom that I wanted, it was similar to that, but it was new, something I didn't have definition for yet. Maybe it wasn't me that wanted freedom, but perhaps it was freedom that wanted me? And they weren't really wings at all on the outside, just that raw joy of living free and alive on the inside, and doing so in the real world and not just my dreams. Founder was teaching me to live from the inside out, and he gradually shoveled away at much of what the world—and I—had buried under piles of lies and pressure.

A homeless man walked by and commandeered my attention from my very important talk with myself—something was unique about him, but at the same time, really, there was nothing that seemed overly unique at all. But perhaps that was the point. He was pushing a cart with a broken wheel, which dragged with a constant hitch. His hair was oily, sparse and stringy, and his skin noticeably rough. But there was something there that I just couldn't put my finger on. I…

"Let's go, Will. Follow me!"

Founder rarely waited to get my attention, and as

usual, led me forward with the sturdy confidence that I would no doubt follow. And I did. He certainly knew all the hunger I still had deep down inside, the kind that keeps too many of us growling for something more, ready to devour a bone clean—usually in the wrong places though. It's insatiable, but it was clear that such bottomless hunger could actually be quite a gift when applied differently—to those unseen places that kept coming alive.

Founder was a few yards ahead of me, nearly bouncing off the heads of the passers-by like a game of hopscotch. He left me on the sidewalk dodging the flood of people coming our way. I knew they couldn't see us, what I didn't know was whether they could feel us, and didn't want to take the chance of bumping into them. Though I was sure I had body checked several amidst the crowd while trying to keep up.

We reached a corner a couple blocks down and took a sharp right. Now I recognized where we were, probably about thirty minutes from my home—downtown Denver. Just ahead stood a sign for the building in front of us: "The Denver Mint." Founder was still staring at the building as he began to speak.

"Here it is Will. Do you recognize it? This is the house from the fourth corner of your nightmare, right?" I looked at him, confused.

"Huh? Are you…do you mean…?"

"Yes, Will. I do. I know you recognize the sign as The Denver Mint, but it means so much more than that. It truly is the mint, but it is also a picture of the oversized house made of money you saw in the fourth corner of your dream."

"You mean nightmare," I said glancing at him. Founder turned his head to the left and began staring back into the flood of people walking down the street. So I looked with him.

He stood still and observed for quite some time, as did I, before looking back towards the mint. He continued to turn his vision from one to the other repeatedly, back and forth without saying a thing, which really insinuated how many things he was preparing to say. I knew he was trying to show me something, which was good. Not only did he keep me on my toes this way, he pushed me to learn to see differently for myself. I noticed a huge difference personally, much better than mere lessons of what's wrong and how to change. With every dream, Founder empowered me not only to see further, but differently, and deeper. My vision was like a toddler who'd never been taught—or allowed—to walk. Now, I was beginning to feel like running.

"Amazing to see the scale of poverty around a house full of money, isn't it?"

I nodded, but didn't speak, just trying to get my mind around what he might be saying, curious where he might be going with it.

"You mean the poverty and the money?" I replied, knowing I was just answering a rhetorical question anyway.

"No, no, no," Founder responded, surprised, "I mean the scale!"

"I don't understand, what scale?"

"The scale of weights and measures. Think about a scale for a second, and I don't mean the type you find in a bathroom. Those weigh you, but there are some related lessons there too I suppose," Founder quipped, laughing gently.

"I'm talking about the old kind of scale, like that which you would have found among your nation's pioneers. The scales that are like a teeter-totter, one side going up, while the other goes down, and vice versa until they are balanced. Do you know the kind I'm talking about?"

I nodded, having seen such tools but never having used one.

"So many people, and much of this nation, have some form of prosperity, even those who are poor, whether they recognize it or not, are often much more wealthy than most of the world. Prosperity is more than mere monetary wealth; it is the flourishing nature of your culture. Your nation has walked in great favor and prosperity, chosen from its beginnings. This is providence. However, the other side of the scale opposite providence is not poverty, as many would suggest. The other side of the scale is people. This nation has a large scale of providence, and people, but has lost its balance. Poverty strikes when our gauge of value falls out of balance."

"Many want to shift that weight, but simply shifting often causes other problems—wide cracks in other ways, like division. The scale would then just keep going up and down, each side constantly reacting to the other. But we were never meant for such a tug-o-war among one another in this nation. Rather, such a rope could be used together to scale the daunting cliffs we might face."

"To return to balance is not a problem of economics, but of mutually esteemed value between people and providence. Value—or the lack there of—is what has tilted the scale and separated providence far away from the people who need it most, now living in a poverty they were never created for, yet carrying a value unseen to too many, including themselves. When you learn to value people, Will, the very people you now look at walking the streets—poor, rich, or otherwise—you create providence, often unknowingly, and begin to shift the scale in your own life while providing momentum for theirs. If you throw your weight at providence, afraid to lose it, that's when people fall into the cracks of poverty—maybe not you, but someone always falls in. But people are the path that actually increases both sides at once. People multiply providence. Aim for providence and splits will happen— much like the culture battles now. Value people, and you've never seen the providence that will be added, even multiplied. People, Will, are this world's greatest resource, not just for their labor; rather, it's their natural worth. This nation knew providence from its birth because of the value it chose to place upon people, near and far. I cannot say this is the case anymore, at least from my vantage point. The quest to sustain providence and power above all else has blinded the eyes of value, and we now see one side of the scale, full of people, crashing downward, and with no wings to re-engage the skies they were created for. But value's eyes can never be taken, only covered. The wolves have succeeded in such for now, but I believe that we, one person at a time, can take back such vision and open the blind eyes to once again see the value waiting to be found in each individual person. Then, Will, providence will dance past midnight once more."

"You see, contrary to what the wolves would have you believe, neither the mint, nor any house of money can tilt the scale back into balance, only people carry enough true weight to balance the nation's collapsing scale. When you value people over providence, you create a spirit of generosity that brings resuscitated life and lift many back into foundations from which they can learn to fly again. Many are relying on the government to split or share the wealth, but you and many others in your mold have much more power than the government does when it comes to sharing the providence you breathe. When the government splits the wealth to correct such imbalance, all you end up with is division, a greater separation between the sides. But when the change comes through the people, one life at a time—especially youth like you—generosity will breed multiplication. Those that you see in the streets back there don't need this house divided among them in order to have more," Founder said while pointing to The Mint, "they need you to begin seeing them and acting towards them with greater value. When you see and value them differently, you will love them differently."

"It is the only way to right the scale, by valuing people over providence. When you learn this—and live this—*you will get both*. Simply, Will, I want you to see this house of money and know that you have more to give those passers by in the streets than this mint could ever offer. You can protect providence in a fearful and self-sustaining way and the imbalance will remain—even grow. Or, you can make generosity the end game through the means of valuing people. That is why I am looking back and forth between these two, the street of people and The Mint. I am asking you, which one do you want, which one will you choose?"

"But Founder," I interjected. "With all due respect, I hear you and I think I understand what you're saying, I really do! But what do I have? I don't know what to even begin to offer such people. I feel like I need what's inside The Mint, before I can even think of looking at them."

"Will, that is the paradox that entraps so many. You forget the value you have inside you—and that which is in them—the power to give what you have in your hands no matter how large or small—such generosity always breeds multiplication, it's contagious!"

"If you don't see the value you possess, in resources that are bigger than money or tangible resources alone, you will never be able to value others the way they need. It is the value in you that brings out the value in them. They don't need your money as much as they need the worth you can prove within them. Prove it every day, anywhere you might go, as if you were reminding someone of the twenty dollar bill pinned to their jacket, so too can you find ways to help them see the value they already carry. Too many people wait to have before they give, but that is the snare of providence; you will never have enough. And often, by the time most have what they deem to be enough, it becomes too difficult to ever let go. Balance the scale between providence and people in your own life, and you will help tip the scale of society, one life at a time. Give what you have, and do so generously, whether treasures, time or talents. It is the generosity, and liberality with which you give your time, your treasures and talents that will show the value you place on others. Will, in my eyes you have far more to give the world than this Mint ever will, or even many

Mints combined. You just have to see yourself correctly, see others through true vision rather than the wolves' facades, and recognize your opportunities. There is a printing press of value inside you, you just have to open the doors for business."

My head was still trying to compute all he said, and implied. What he said made a lot of sense actually, and felt very empowering, but how was I supposed to know where to start? That was the biggest issue in our house. I stood by too many days watching my parents unknowingly tear new and bigger cracks in our family through their arguments and frustration with the economy. I'd heard endless news and debate about it over the years, and yet, I don't think I actually ever *heard* anything. What Founder said scared the living daylights out of me, but something inside me also told me he was right. My parents argued over the power of the government and who was taking their providence, but no one had ever valued the power I had in my life—until Founder.

"Will, have you ever looked closely at the back of the one dollar bill?"

He was on a roll, and could barely stop long enough to let me breathe, let alone think. But maybe I was just supposed to listen. So I re-focused.

"Yeah, I guess I have."

"No, Will, I don't think you're understanding what I am truly asking you. Have you really ever *seen* what is on the back of a dollar bill to understand what it might mean?"

"I guess I haven't then." That apparently was the answer Founder had assumed, and was waiting to hear.

"Do you have one?" Founder asked as he lit up like a Christmas light.

"Nah, sorry. I didn't bring my wallet with me," I said with a laugh.

However, Founder seemed less than amused. He was too focused and already clearly moving on about our business.

"That's fine, don't worry about it. I'll just describe it to you. But next time you see one, take a look at what I'm about to tell you."

"On the back of the dollar bill there is a seal with two statements, one on top and the other on bottom. The first statement you will find over the pyramid says, 'Annuit Coeptus,' which basically means, 'Providence favors our beginnings or endeavors.' Remember that. And below the pyramid on the great seal is a statement which reads, 'Novus Ordo Seclorum,' which is also Latin and means 'New order for generations.' Do you know what this means, Will?"

I didn't say a word, but just kept listening.

"Many scrutinize the literal meanings, or are suspicious of secretive, coded meanings. But I want to really look at what they *can* mean to you, to us, regardless of anyone else's intent," he let out with a gust. "If providence favors our endeavors, and especially new beginnings—which by the way is what much of the American dream was originally built on—then all we must do is take such providence and direct it towards those who really need it, using providence not to inflate our pride, but for the sake of valuing others. That's how the formal nature of our nation began, with many testimonies of such, not always perfectly, but the intent was there. We can use the providence of this nation for more than defining 'the dream,' but as a means to launch ourselves and others back into new orbit. That's where value peeks in again and reminds the caterpillars whom they really are, with butterfly wings just waiting to surprise, and beautifully emerge. Providence is a means, not an end. We are trying to use our providence to create more providence, but we're not empowering all the empty souls who have room in their lives to hold and share it, they are where our increase waits to be known. We spend all this time to multiply and increase our providence, but it only multiplies through people, the very people we're letting slip into the imbalanced crack of poverty. When those such as you take the riches of this nation—beyond the monetary and from our deepest motives—and invest in one another, we will put in motion a new order that will affect generations to come, one new beginning at a time. A new, hopeful order will emerge from a path laid brick by brick, stone by stone, of one new beginning at a time. If we truly have the providence the great seal declares, ironically written upon money itself, then what is to stop you from using such providence to make people your endeavor, and give as many new beginnings as humanly possible, the very kind of new beginning you yourself have too often longed for? How can you ask for such, but be unwilling to invest in others for the very same?"

As I thought about it, I couldn't help but imagine back to the image of the homeless man that was still engrained upon my heart.

"But Founder, look how so many people who are in need use, and even abuse, what is given to them. They use it to drink, or in other harmful ways that just dig deeper holes and waste what is given. How do I know if there is a change from what I give? How do I know that they have felt the difference?"

"That's a great question, Will. And to be honest, you cannot know for sure. You can't control change in their lives, but you can control it in your own. The key to generosity is not just to give until they feel it; it is learning to give until you feel it. That is the only way to guarantee change. You cannot control their end result, but you can choose how you live and may determine the mark you leave on their lives, whether they recognize it or not. It is not called generosity because someone receives something in a big way, but because of how it is given."

Founder quieted himself while I continued soaking it in, realizing I had a thick head full of old thinking for all this to seep through. But truly, no matter how foreign this was to me, he was right. I couldn't control change in others, but I could change what I controlled. I started picturing the dollar bill and the statements Founder described. I didn't remember ever reading them intently, but I would surely go back to them now. I remembered different conspiracies about them, but that was just another thing, true or not, that wasn't mine to control. But I would determine their power through my life.

Despite my lack of familiarity with the words, it was easy to remember the picture of an eagle, like...

"No, Will, it's not me," Founder interrupted the question arising in my head, and without hesitation. "I actually get that question a lot. The eagle on the back of the dollar isn't me, but it is my great, great grandfather, and I do carry his name." Founder smirked at me, inspiring my own curious grin to pop up.

"And there is another Latin statement in that seal with his picture as well. It says, 'E Pluribus Unum.' It means that out of many, come one. Many people are afraid of this. They are afraid of the scale being changed to one pot in order to rectify the balance. Many fear that such free living and giving will take what they have and divide it into many parts, never to see it again, a dangerous false hope when administered rather than empowered. But if you, and many others like you will indeed one at a time take such power back through your lives, and begin to live with an overriding value and generosity towards one another, the scales of providence and people will again become one, and that's when they both will grow and rise together. That's how many will come together from many different vantage points to become one—through a different sort of value. Value people, and you will get providence thrown in. Overvalue providence, and eventually you will get neither. It's not about which side is right, it's becoming level in a way that removes the cracks of poverty and helps us all rise together, as one. We were once one nation, but our great strength of providence has become one of our greatest weaknesses and has led to division as we forgot what led us into such a dream. We won't see the strength of our gift revived until true value, through people, is once again esteemed."

I turned around and began walking in a way I never had with Founder. Usually, he led me. But he had unearthed a different value in me, from me, and for others as well. I so desperately wanted hope, but I was beginning to think I might not find it apart from giving it. So I walked from our place before The Mint directly towards where we started, amid the sea of people on the streets. I felt not only a new hope, I felt a fire in my eyes looking to ignite someone else—even one. I hadn't been entirely truthful with Founder, which I assumed he knew. My monthly allowance was in my back pocket, dream or no dream. And though I truly didn't think a one-dollar bill was included, as I had responded before, the reality was I didn't think I got a big enough allowance to give. But that's not where I was counting my worth anymore. It wasn't whether I had enough, but whether I was enough. The twenty dollar bill was in my pocket, but it wasn't an amount as much as fuel for my fire, fuel to take what I had and let someone feel such warmth in the ways they might need it most, which I assumed would be different in every interaction. My perspective's new beginning could offer the very same to another's reality.

My heart was a stampede, leaving the soil underneath both ripe and raw. Founder chased slowly, watching from behind. Unseen as before, I took the money from behind me, plucked the pen from my side and started to scribble on the bill; "You are valued!!!!!" I could have kept adding exclamations but ran out of room. There, again, was the man from before. Just as homeless, but in my eyes now ripe. He was probably just as so before, but even that which is ripe has to wait for someone who is ready to do the picking. I walked over just behind where he was sprawled out on the concrete, where a guitar case lay instrument-less, change-less too. I stood from his back and dropped the bill from my once grasping pinch and let it flutter down to him as if a gift from above. I scurried over to a bench a mere fifteen feet to his right, while Founder joined me now latched firmly on my shoulder.

The man couldn't see me, but I could see him. So I watched.

For more than an hour I waited for him to awake. Every time he stirred I'd feel my insides get all nervous and excited. It was only twenty dollars to some, but again, the amount didn't matter. I was going all in on someone who did matter.

When he finally woke up, he gave me a gift I'll never forget. He plucked the bill from his case and held it to the light of the sky, then immediately flipped it around to find my small note competing for his attention with the "two zero's" all around the bill's corners. He smiled. The old man smiled in a way that gave me life. He was touched, but not more so than me. With his cart left behind I watched him walk to the convenience store across the street. And my fear started to rise. What if he...no, I couldn't go there. That's not what this was about. And out he came, at first to my chagrin, with two unfortunate beverages of choice, and two sandwiches in hand. I wasn't expecting what happened next though. Instead of crossing back to his cart, he veered off track and knelt by the man sleeping on the bench across the street. He stirred him hard until the younger man shook off what the nights and days had left him. And I will never forget watching this younger man's thankfulness as he handed a sandwich, and yes, one of the beverages of choice. I realized more than ever, I couldn't always make the right decision for someone else, but I could give imperfectly until it mattered, and watch others imperfectly do the same.

The two men finished their meals together, and the older man simply walked away from the younger. They may not have known one another, but they knew well that which one another battled through. A homeless man gave from his nothing, but in doing so helped cover up the cracks—even if only a little—for someone else. I'd long experienced a lack of hope. More than ever did I realize that alone was my qualification to give hope to many, many more. Perhaps that by itself would be my hope—or a large part nonetheless. I could take the battles fought and won in my own life to bring hope to others.

Chapter 14:
The Tenth Dream: Scars

"America will never be destroyed from the outside. If we falter and lose our freedoms, it will be because we destroyed ourselves." - Abraham Lincoln

The waves crashed violently, but there was amid such an air of complete peace. I always loved that about the ocean. The sand was wet and rugged, not smooth like many other beaches. It was an overcast day and the clouds were so low it seemed they were trying to sneak their way towards the ground. This wasn't a sunny touristy beach, but much more secluded, and it held somewhat of a rainy, mountainous feel. There were but a few people in sight, one jogger, someone walking their dog and a woman reading on a far-off boulder. The seagulls were typically lively and the ocean swallowed up most of the other noises, which I was thankful for. There are few other sounds that captivate me more than that of the crashing waves. I rarely get to experience the sound other than on CD or DVD myself. I could sit here all day.

"Me too!" Founder chimed in. "This is one of my favorite places on earth. I look back, I look forwards, and each perspective becomes that much more rich because of the peace in the moment. When I am here, I can take it all in and process life and thought in ways I'm often not ready for in the moment. Being here always recaptures those moments well, and allows me to breathe through them in ways I can't always seem to elsewhere."

"Hmm, I get that, Founder, but you had told me not to be defined by looking back in the past. I remember it well actually because I've had to really work not to since you said it, I suppose realizing how much I naturally do it."

"Well, yes Will, I did say that. But the key there is not to avoid the past, rather it's understanding how not to be defined by it. You can be empowered by the past if you look back in the right way, for the right reasons."

"Your past can be one of the most powerful tools you have to share and give to others when it is full of stories, journeys and even difficulties that you've overcome. Like looking at a scar on your body, you can't feel the pain anymore, nor peel the scab. But you can enjoy what they now reflect, and the stories they still tell."

As he spoke of such scars, I couldn't help but let my mind wander a little. Thinking back into my own life made me wonder if I had any scars. Or maybe, mine weren't healed just yet and only told half a story. And if they weren't scars yet, I now knew that they were at least finally on their way to such, hopefully speaking that is.

"Founder, do you really have scars? You seem so wise, I mean, you *are* so wise. It doesn't seem like someone such as you would put yourself in that kind of danger."

"Will, it's not about danger, it is life. Where do you think such wisdom comes from if not for scars?"

I started to well up with tears, like all my insides could feel the depth, the reality, and yet the power of his words. It was comforting to hear.

"Scars reveal a lot of hidden truth, Will, which is just one more resource you have to live with and generously give out. Scars are stories that bring life."

The wells in my eyes were getting a little too full now to contain the emotion I felt imagining what Founder was saying. It was true in my own life; I just hoped I might make the most of all that the pain has caused.

"Founder, what is your story?" I asked. "I know you've shared it in increments, when necessary that is, but about your scars, I want to understand."

He began to shuffle in his stance, like he was settling in, not out of discomfort but as a wise Grandfather might while preparing to settle into the grooves of wisdom's seat.

"That's a very long answer, Will, but I suppose we can take the first bite. I come from a line of eagles that held great favor in this nation. Your culture has always known us for the heights we soared, the dreams we believed, the incredible vision we possessed and for the freedom we represented. But I started to take it all for granted. Please don't get me wrong; I hadn't abandoned such principles, and I still very much wanted what they had to offer. But, I slowly fell into a trap that even I could not recognize. The nation was united, the economy was flourishing, and I was coming into my own. However, with everything looking up on the outside I forgot to keep rising up from the inside. That's the thing about freedom, Will. It is most powerful from the inside out. I fell in love with the freedom I became accustomed to, and slowly, forgot how to live true freedom on the inside. It dulled my vision, and I became too apathetic to rise to the heights needed to truly live that dream anymore. Have you heard of that phrase, Will?"

"Which one is that?"

"*Living the dream.* Have you heard that said before? A lot of people respond like such when asked how they're doing—'living the dream.' I know we've danced around that phrase in our own adventures, but I ask that, Will, because I often wonder if they really are. I wonder if most people even know what that dream is anymore? Otherwise, it seems those dreams are just to measure up with everyone else, and the standards the wolves have set. In reality, there is no singular dream, there can't be as it would be contrary to the very premise. So when I hear that statement I almost cringe, as it often means someone has fallen into the sheep culture with low expectations of how said dream could be defined. If they were truly living the dream, there would be a different dream to describe for each person, extending far beyond that phrase. 'Life, liberty, and the pursuit of happiness' does not equal house, car, and a high paying job. To live the dream is less about words and definition, and in fact less about externals as a whole. To live the dream is at least as much pursuit as it is happiness; to have your wings fully spread, from the inside out, to live your freedom towards a goal more than possess it as your goal."

He finished with a whip out to each side, spreading his wings wider and more open than I had ever seen them before. With a big-beaked but somber smile, he opened his feathers and I became wide-eyed with shock. There he was, one like Founder, and his wings looked almost to be defaced top to bottom in scars—like he had been torn to shreds without stop. I couldn't help but start to well up with tears again, as I couldn't imagine how he'd survived such an obvious massacre, let alone what all the scars, as he'd said earlier, might mean. What had he gone through? How had he survived it? When did it happen, and by whom? My mouth was still agape surveying them all. This noble eagle that epitomized such virtues to so many—*as well as myself*—had nearly lost his wings, or at least his ability to fly it appeared after looking at the wreckage done. And yet, now, I already knew the short end of the answer, for I had never seen any eagle fly higher.

"What you say is true, Will. I have never flown higher than when my scars healed. My wings were more stalwart and able than ever before, and I flew to heights I had spoken of, but had never actually been. That was living the dream!"

I sat in silence, still trying to process his scars. It wasn't one or two after all. He was covered; a litany of pain clearly spelled out in his own excruciating language, yet obviously now translated back into a dialect of hope. I had to know.

"Founder," I spoke softly, "what happened?"

"Will, you remember the glass box from your nightmare? Well, I let a box like that slowly take over my own life while it masqueraded as a dream. But the dream I thought I'd possessed was far from real, fleeting at best. I fell from the heights I once flew, and such a box could not have contained me had I not passively permitted it to. The thing of it is, Will, I possessed all the traits I represented because of the heights that I flew at, and the heights those before me soared to as well. But, slowly, and without realizing it, I began to value the heights I was associated with over the flying that lifted me there in the first place. The two seem to go hand in hand, and it was a subtle decision, like spending counterfeit money. But it was far more costly. I almost forgot how to fly. Then, temporarily at least, I almost lost my ability to."

"Founder, I don't get it. How is that even possible? You fly so naturally, it doesn't seem like that could be taken from you, it's in your nature as an eagle."

"Yes, but I forgot who I was—who I truly am—and I traded it for the esteem of life rather than the dreams of actually living it."

I put up my hands, motioning him to hold on. "Founder, I hear what you're saying, but how?"

"As you well know by now, Will, my line of eagles has been the symbol for much of what your culture was originally built from, and for. Eventually, when it was my time, I became the face of such freedom and vision. Before this, I flew high and dreamed big. I didn't even know the heights I flew to because that wasn't my goal. The only desire I had then was to fully enjoy being who I was made to be, and to fly high in my dreams, challenging the heights, not to attain them, but to keep dreaming. *That was living the dream!* But when it was my turn to rise up in stature, I lowered myself in truth and freedom. I was given the high perch that my family had always sat on, to be a symbol of such a glorious nation and such powerful beliefs. But I gave up living those beliefs to sit on that high perch. This wasn't just any perch, it was high-profile, and something most only dream of, but few get the chance to find out that there isn't much of a dream there at all, only a counterfeit life. I became a counterfeit version of myself, and all freedom's possibilities within me."

"That perch was the ultimate height in others' opinion, might as well have been the oval office. But it was the lowest I had flown in years, since I was a very young eagle. Everything that is associated with eagles such as me: vision, freedom, and so much more all stems from the internal truth that those characteristics are naturally alive in us, they are innate. We don't need anyone to affirm us as eagles to actually be one; it's already in us. But in a sheep culture, too many too often fall for trying to live up to *the* dream while leaving their own natural wings to lie dormant at their side. You can count sheep at night, but don't ever dream with them or before you know it you'll aim for what the wolves trick them to behold."

"Will, I gave up my flying to sit on that desired perch. Instead of soaring high and free, I lowered myself to a glorious branch that was engraved with gold, embossed with the very words that I once actually lived. Under where I sat my perch read: 'Freedom, Vision, Providence, and many such similar virtues and values, many of which you and I have discussed at length. Essentially, I traded the dreams of flying for the definition of an esteemed title. The sheep gathered around me and they listened. They never knew me when I flew so high and free, but it was back then that I actually did represent all they thought I was."

"The sheep began to worship the freedom I represented, and freedom is great, but to them it was a concept to be possessed rather than a life to be lived. And I wasn't doing a sufficient job showing them otherwise either. I don't know if my perch got lower and lower, or if the sheep kept building their pasture higher, but before I knew it I couldn't tell the difference between the skies and the path to slaughter, then everything changed. I never wanted such change, and I had no idea how my own counterfeit living was actually making the box all around us draw in smaller by the day. I was reinforcing the box with my life and actions, and I even put a lid on it with my perch."

"My wings grew heavy, I hadn't truly flown in years. Sure I had my token flights, drifting around the box no higher than the perch, and this lasted for so long that I didn't even know what I was missing anymore, always quick in justification, convincing myself such a lukewarm dream could even be described as a dream. I was so caught up being the picture of the sheep's dreams that I lost my own when I actually could have inspired true ideals in them. Now that I look back, I could have written a totally different story through their lives, and the best thing I could have done—I could have empowered them in the true freedom that had gone incognito, locked up inside me. They got a mascot, as I might as well have been painted red, white and blue, but we all lost such a tri-colored life, and yet, I could have shown them otherwise. I left far more scars upon them than my own wings could show you now; simply by inhibiting the more I knew to be possible for them each. My vision was waning as well. It became more dull by the day, so much so that even I couldn't see what was still alive inside me—albeit hidden and on life support."

"Will, my perch became so low that the sheep started to realize that my so-called freedom they believed I held all those years was non-existent anymore. I was now a lie in my very own truth. They began to argue and riot, until I realized…" Founder put his head down and began to sob almost uncontrollably. But they weren't tears of pain or discomfort, at least they didn't seem like it. Founder cried big, deep, passionate tears resembling grief and anguish, the tears of his scars, which as he had so eloquently put it, had turned to wisdom. I had never seen someone grieve like this before. You would have thought he was at his own funeral, but still with lots of new beginnings.

"I realized they weren't sheep anymore, but wolves. It was a quiet and almost underground change, but it was very real. That is how I got the wounds that became these scars," he said while lifting up his wings again, once more exposing the depth of his former pain. I gulped deep down inside, not knowing what to say.

"They tore me apart. They fought over the freedom they thought I possessed, the words written under me all those years. The words I stopped modeling too long before. The most apathetic of sheep became the most terrifying of wolves, simply because I failed to point out what could have been alive from within them. I could have given them wings and shown them the way out of the box. With wings, there's no need for a perch, or such an empty pursuit. I could have made them honorary eagles and led them into the true freedom that they could choose each day. I could have brought to life the unique and eternally free treasures that were hidden in their hearts. *That* is why I grieve today. I bowed to their dream and the heights they esteemed instead of flying high and showing them a better way. I don't grieve for what those wolves did to me, nearly ending all I was. I grieve because I became more sheep than eagle, which made them more and more like wolves."

"I ache deeply under each of these scars because they remind me of every sheep I led astray. Each scar reminds me of the sheep like you who are being devoured by a culture of wolves, while your heart dreams to be an eagle that truly sees—who lives out the freedom within you. Had I flown high in the presence of those sheep, the very reason they looked up to us in the first place, I would have given them a hope that could not be contained. Soon, one by one, they would have developed wings of their own. I could have given hope fresh air in their lives—and yours. Will, I'm not here to help you avoid the wolves, rather, I want you to become like the eagle this nation came to honor. Neither you, nor your family, nor the nation need a mascot that sums up what you once had. You each need lives that reflect a glimmer of those skies for yourselves. If you live for yourself you will become a sheep, exterminating true freedom one chemical at a time, no matter how noble your principles and values for such are. If you truly live what things like freedom and vision mean, then you will realize they aren't something to be possessed, but to be fuel for your wings, to be the very skies that draw out such a yearning you can't help but launch out and discover that believing is seeing, it requires first flight to know those skies exist anymore. There are many different kinds of eagles, or at least there should be. Only some will carry the identity of an eagle, but all can live out what the spirit of the eagle represents. Isn't that the very spirit that was declared and signed by the original founders of this nation?"

"When you become the picture of hope for your nation you won't just live the dream, you will break open the boxes that are suffocating the dreams of others. Every sheep naturally goes one way or the other. There is no staying a sheep, nor becoming a more successful sheep, no matter what anyone tells you. A sheep is a sheep because they follow direction, but in the direction they choose they are transformed by slaughter or the skies. There are only two choices outside of feeling led to slaughter; you will slowly become a wolf as a defense, or start flying high like an eagle in your own hope-crafting purpose. There is no middle ground, Will. The perch most sheep stare at and strive for is actually no perch at all, but that doesn't stop men from relentlessly building their ladders of success to reach there. I found that out the hard way. You need no ladder; I want you to fly, Will! I want you not just to dream of dreams, but to live them and give the same hope to many more. I want you to take the scars that have made you cry out, the very pain that brought my attention and let them become part of your culture's healing. I want you to fly higher than I ever have. I want you to see truths that are unseen by the masses. I want you to be an eagle, not over a nation of sheep, but who inspires and strengthens the spirited but wounded wings of other soon-to-be sky dwellers."

I shook my head in disbelief, and my insides started quaking with tears, though I didn't know if I had any tears left to give after the streams that had been running down my face while he spoke. I was still young, but I had fallen for so many of these traps already, and even if they'd been to a lesser degree, I could only imagine how many more I might have been headed towards. But I would not compromise anymore, and hopefully not ever again. Not at home, not at school, and not in the dreams I *was* pursuing.

"I was a figurehead for a nation of sheep, so I became the dinner of wolves." Founder said, with a nod towards me.

"Now, I lead people in their dreams!"

Chapter 15:
Dreaming of Home

"The measure of intelligence is the ability to change."
- Albert Einstein

When I woke up from the time Founder and I spent at the beach I realized something that had been building in me throughout my times with my wise friend. Before that first dream, I was desperate for an answer of hope. But Founder taught me something, well, he taught me many things. But it was that morning I realized I didn't just want hope, but I wanted a true home. I had a desire within me much stronger than I had ever allowed to surface before. I wanted something new in the family and world that surrounded me, and I had started to resent those who seemingly weren't cooperating. And while I had been wishing for some sort of hope to come to me, it had instead been made clear to me that hope, like many things, was much more a means than an end. Hope would be the means, and maybe, a true home would be the end. I could no longer wait for others to have better answers to offer me any more than my parents could argue over politics, I had to live the better answers towards them. I can still see that morning like it was yesterday, and yet still learning from it today.

****

"Will, time for breakfast!" Mom yelled towards my room as she headed down the stairs, likely on her way to boil some eggs.

"I'm down here, Mom," I answered as she turned the corner.

"What are you doing?" she asked in an almost agitated tone, though probably just a little taken back by the moment. I didn't read into her tone though, it's not as if she found me here often. I looked up at her while making breakfast, with the type of smile that rarely graced my mouth. The bacon crackled and let off a smell more revealing than if she could see it on the stove, which was good, because she wasn't looking at the stove. She was still turning circles in the doorway, a quizzical look on her face, mouth agape and glaring at all the open windows.

I had gotten up early that morning, and the first thing I did was draw open all the blinds and curtains my family and I too often hid behind. What better way to speak to the home I wanted than to let fresh light flood in that it might speak for me, offer some new perspective or just to reveal the views of the towering mountain peaks out west? Though I think they were just masquerading as mountains, I knew them now for what they had become within me; monuments of hope. I secretly wondered which one held the ridge Founder and I had stood upon.

Even the bacon, as simple as it may sound, was a new twist to the morning. That was usually saved only for the weekends, and rarely cooked on the stove. I went back to cutting some fresh fruit and Mom followed, I think still trying to figure me out, or perhaps she thought she was in her own dream. She hovered over my shoulder but I didn't sense any concern, nor was there any of that weighty feeling that she sometimes carried with her, and often measured down on me. I felt more like she was trying to understand, if that makes sense. To be honest, she seemed a little bewildered and that probably made more sense than I did, compared to usual, that is.

She looked tired, worn, simply trying to get up and get going for another push of a day that all too frequently lacked joy, bearing the heaviness of survival. I set a place for her and I at the table. Dad had already left for work, and David wasn't up yet.

While I finished making breakfast she couldn't help

herself from gazing into the light that was blaring through the window onto the table, you would have thought she'd be used to it in sunny Colorado. But just because the sun was out in the morning, it didn't always mean Mom could see, or feel it. I knew how that felt, and was realizing it's actually pretty easy to do something as simple as partner with the sun. It might have seemed superficial, but I watched how much power had been locked up in such a minute change. I knew she didn't block out the light on purpose, it's more likely the blinds stayed closed out of simple habit. That's what survival will do to you, or so I'd been told. It's amazing how those frivolous habits can become such powerful, thieving cycles in our lives. Those were the real windows that—one at a time—I was looking to open.

That morning for breakfast we still had eggs. I didn't want to get too hasty. But, I decided to scramble them and even add a little cheese. A couple pieces of bacon seemed to project more strength than the protein they could truly offer, resembling an upward curved bridge on the plate and leading right up to the fresh fruit. "Fresh" was the word I couldn't help but think of over and again. It was the word I wanted Mom to feel. I had even grabbed the usual snacks she would take for her own lunch at work: a simple yogurt, water and a half sandwich.

"Oh, I almost forgot the coffee!"

That one perked my mom right up before she could take a sip. She even cracked a smile, and the cool thing is it wasn't smearing off all that easy. From that moment on, she kept smiling. She got up from her seat and jogged up the stairs with surprising energy. Next thing I knew she was walking down with David, holding his hand and apparently wanting to let him in on this new revelation. I was learning quickly that it really didn't take much for change to begin.

I was still kind of dumbfounded by it all, finding these little changes mutually easy, and hard. I hadn't really done anything that any other family might do any old day. But, I did change my perspective and so far it seemed to be oiling the smallest of hinges in our home. Not only that, but it was multiplying. I watched Mom bring David into the room. She clearly loves David, but often struggles to have patience for his battles while at the same time fighting her own. But, joyfully, she began to do for him the very things I had just done for her. Again, it wasn't so much about what she did on his behalf as much as the perspective she'd apparently caught. Light had invaded our home, far more so than what came through the windows. David smiled the calmest, most real smile I had seen cross his face in some time. He sat up tall as if he just found out he grew an inch. The light was more subtly contagious than I thought. Mom and David both seemed renewed.

"Do you want me to drive you boys to school today?" she asked willingly, I actually saw some want-to in her eyes.

David and I looked at each other, "Yeaaahhhh!!" David yelled, beating me to the punch. We finished our breakfast and all romped around the house in a loud, unusual manner as we prepared for the day. There was something alive to it all, it lacked that stale, burnt coffee smell that some of our less-than routines could so easily generate. And Mom didn't close any of the blinds either. She left all the windows open for the house to simmer in the sun all day—like Grandma's crock-pot I thought to myself, fondly remembering that small town feel, and smell. As we drove to school, I started wondering how I could live out the same changes towards those around me in the classrooms and halls all day; surely not an easy task, but a worthwhile one.

I stepped into the hallway, like I did every morning, but this time was different. I was going to make it different. Those halls were the dark tunnel I sprinted to get out of each day, but this day, I was looking for that one small crack that might let me bring the light inside. Never had I started a school day with this kind of perspective, and that alone would cause change. Even if for no one else, at least I'd know I began the path my heart was laying out for me. I knew I might not be able to control how those around me responded, this was still high school after all, and I braced myself for the reality that not everyone might see the light as Mom witnessed earlier that morning, and still some might have a measure of this light already that I could glean from, or at least I hoped so. Such a pursuit of hope might have been a little too utopian for many of them, at least for the time being. But, that wasn't going to stop me. I could see the glimmers trying to sneak their way in and knew that meant I had to learn to maintain view of each of those small rays, even while in the dark. More than ever, I had this inner resolve not to conform another day to the lagging hope that hung heavily around the neck of so many of those around me, waiting for more prey to step under its yoke.

I wasn't prey anymore, more like a bird of prey I thought, daydreaming of Founder now and what he would say to us if he could be the one teaching first period history. Then I'd actually be looking forward to class. I transitioned at my locker to start the day and was enraptured in thoughts and dreams, imagining I had Founder's eyes, or at least his vision. In one way, even I thought I was a little cuckoo. But Founder was becoming so vivid to me—all around me—and I wanted to learn to see with those piercing eyes of his, the vision that could capture and extract treasures from the darkest and most buried of places—and people. And, I was determined to see through that smog of so-called "normal reality," whatever that was supposed to be. I wanted to live out the reality that there really is powerful, hidden truth inside me that others needed too, no matter how long it takes to see them infected. I wanted to live by, and towards, the very same in them as well. I imagined hope infiltrating the school—one life at a time—and wondered what could be if they too were partakers of my reinterpreted dream.

There was a different way to live available to us all, so how could I keep it a secret? Perhaps little had changed for me on the outside, yet! But I already felt the better life.

There was an eagle soaring inside that had mentored me anew, and would lead me into skies of limitless possibility, just above the dim clouds of supposed reality. There was more, and it was spelled out through different means all around me just waiting to be found. *There is more.* More than boiled eggs, more than "the dream" of sheep, even more than my very own hope. Even though I was now convinced, I still needed to keep expanding, rising higher like a balloon filled with anything but hot air. And I don't think I had even begun to taste it yet, not even in the bacon. I wasn't there yet, but I had set myself free to begin and to believe my way down that newly uncovered path.

Starry-eyed and shuffling through the crowded hallway I got bumped and shoved as usual. My books were knocked from my hands before I could reach my first class, yet my grip still felt stronger than ever. Very little changed throughout the day, at least that I could see. But I was undeterred. Hope was undeterred. I wanted to be like Founder and leave whatever perch I was on, or hoping to climb, and begin re-exploring the skies, expanding society beyond where feet already traveled; revealing the sheep for *who* they really are—or could be.

But there was one thing I realized that day. Though I

stayed positive and hopeful amidst the perpetual challenges projected and hurled my direction, despite my day's good intentions, I still struggled with how to live it out in the moment. But then again, maybe it wasn't about the moment. Maybe it was more like that deep breath Founder kept reminding me of as he led me out of my nightmare. Maybe it would take time, persistent and consistent time. No longer was I a sheep among wolves, being lulled into their slaughter. I was a baby eagle among them just learning how to stumble awkwardly out of my nest and truly fly. It was one thing to see my mom experience change through my simple acts of the morning. But I still wanted to open the windows and make breakfast for the rest of those all around me. As I learned that morning, waking up much earlier than the norm, a good breakfast takes time to cook.

Little did I know a surprise was waiting for me later that afternoon at home, a quickened harvest from the seeds planted that morning, and in the most unlikely soil, but perhaps the most needy and receptive. A quiet knock on my still cracked open door showed me David standing in its threshold. Normally, I would have been quick to slam that crack the rest of the way, and fling its lock into secure position. I rarely looked for the patience I'd need to mine for hope in David, which was probably on me much more than him or the challenges he might carry into my space. But David had a presence about him I'd rarely felt. He was peaceful, at least for him. There wasn't that electric charge, or combustible moment waiting to happen that he so often lived with, welcome or not. There was something raw, and almost hope filled about the way he peered through that crack, as if now he was the light trying to break into the dark. "Will, can I come in?"

"Sure, David. Of course." Though the 'of course' probably wasn't a fair choice of words, seeing as my favorable response wasn't very common. "What's up, bud?" I asked as I sat back, leaning relaxed against the wall.

"Umm, uh...I, oh, I don't know, forget it. I, I'll just see you at dinner." Arms straight down by his side, David turned, head down, timidly walking back out the crack in the door he came through.

"Wait, David, come on back, please. Really. What's going on?"

"Uhh, III...III, I don't know exactly. I just feel different, but I don't know why. And then, um, well, Will, you seem different." I interrupted him there, though I think he was at a stopping point anyway, still so mellow though. I was amazed that he was so apt to sense what was happening. For all of his challenges, David is incredibly perceptive, even if he doesn't always know how to relay the sonar like messages he's picking up.

"What are you feeling, David? Is it inside, or outside? What started it? Was it this morning when Mom got you up for breakfast?"

"Well, kind of. But there's more. I had a dream."

"Wait, wait, what kind of dream? What was it about? There didn't happen to be a large eag…" David interrupted me this time.

"It was you, Will. You were in the dream, just you and me. But we weren't here at home either. It was, uh, it was kinda weird. We were at the zoo! But I can't remember the last time we even went to the zoo."

I laughed out loud. Wondering if I really did know what he was going to speak next. But then it occurred to me. "David, you said it was only you and I at the zoo? There was no one else? And I mean, *no one* else?"

"Well, yeah, there were a few animals actually, but that's it." I sighed with a slight smile.

"You mean there was an eagle, huh David?"

"Nope, no eagle at all. That would've been cool though! It was you and I, and, well, a bunch of sheep. But that's what made it so weird, and I think why you were there. You saved me!" He blurted out, actually starting to cry. "Will, I thought they were sheep, but, bbbuh, but, they, they…"

"They were wolves?"

"Yes! How did you know?"

"Are you sure there was no eagle at all? It wasn't a large, fatherly bird that saved you?

"Will, why do you keep asking about an eagle? It was you! Is that how you knew about the wolves? What's going on? Right after you pulled me away from the wolves, you were about to say something. You had this real serious look, but kind of this funny smirk too. But that's when Mom woke me up. Will, what were you going to tell me?" I paused for a few moments, not sure what, if, or how much to dive into.

"It was just a dream, pal. Don't worry about it. Maybe we can talk about it more later."

"No, Will, now! It wasn't just a dream, it was real and you know it. How else would you have known about the wolves? I know it was real!" David was pretty riled up now, which was much more like I was used to. But it was still different, he was riled up about a conviction deep down inside. Even though I might have processed it differently, I had felt it before. However, I didn't know what to say. Why was I the one in the dream instead of Founder? What was I supposed to tell him? But, regardless of my questions, David was right. It wasn't just a dream. How he knew that I don't know, but that's the part I needed to pay attention to. Not the *how* necessarily, just the fact that he knew.

David's dream made me realize that something in him, same as what had been in me, was now crying out. I often didn't give David the credit or value he deserved, but I wasn't alone either. He has a diagnosis, one of those that starts with that big letter "A." I'd rather not say which one to you because I don't want to add to that unfair label. It's not who he is. I've learned that now. He is so much more than any diagnosis. There's a dream inside of him, that now, even he knows is more than a dream. It's real. It's a hope that the world around him needs. He just needed someone who'll look for that dream in him long enough to bring it to the surface. But in saying such, it made me wonder all the more why Founder wasn't there. Why was it me who took Founder's place with the sheep, and the wolves? I didn't feel ready for something of that magnitude. I looked back over at David, who was waiting patiently for a response. "Are you sure it was me, David? Are you sure I was the one who pulled you up on that overlooking bridge?"

David smiled back at me unusually happy. "It was you, Will. I know that. But I never told you about the bridge. See, you know the dream I'm talking about! You were there!" I didn't say anything else. I put my arm around my little brother, took a deep breath, and gave in nodding in agreement. He lit up with a new spark, and bounced out of the room without another question, for that day at least. David had seen hope, and it was now bigger than any circumstance or diagnosis that was trying to box him in.

Chapter 16:
The Final Dream:
Philadelphia

"Hope is a waking dream." - Aristotle

Founder had apparently been waiting for me while I passed through my dreams. As I arrived on the scene it was largely unfamiliar territory, except for one glaring object I had seen and heard about on many occasions—*The Liberty Bell*. We were in Philadelphia.

Founder himself looked renewed, freshly groomed and strong in countenance. Not that I had ever noticed anything to the contrary prior to this, but he appeared to have an extra brightness and strength about him.

Renewed was the only word I could think of. Oh, how I'd come to love these escapes with him. I couldn't fully put words as to why, but my heart naturally went to a posture of reminiscing over such adventures, replaying them in my mind for my life to learn. Founder was more than a mentor or a guide; he was a close friend, and probably even more like a father. It was his deep love that set me free to relate to him as one. I don't know if I had ever been around an elder who made sure I felt that much love and appreciation. I knew my parents loved me, but they were in their own hard place. Founder didn't have to say the words, and to be honest I don't think he ever had spoken those words to me out loud, but he didn't have to, he communicated in so many other forms.

Looking upon him now, I couldn't help but think back to the bed of scars on his wings he had revealed on the beach. Every scar had clearly made him stronger, and now, he flew higher than ever, like each one was a tune-up. What's more, I think I too was finally starting to fly. Perhaps not literally, but my spirit was soaring. I could see the effects on my home and family from the day before, even in the smallest ways. But still, I loved these dreams. This is where I got filled up; where I could find the adventures I'd been hoping for and take a deep breath from the reality of my day.

"How is your family doing, Will?" Founder interjected.

"Pretty well, I suppose. Yesterday was a good day,

especially with my mom and brother; hoping for a lot more of those. Actually, to even use the word hope in regards to us feels like pretty amazing progress to me. And really, I just wish they could meet you for themselves. Would really do them some good."

"Perhaps they can, Will. But you will have to introduce us of course."

"Yes! I'd love to! I was just asking David if he had met you, he started to dream, you know. Just tell me how. Will it be in their sleep? Should I have them crash for the night in my room, would that help? Just point me the way, please."

"OK, but to tell you the truth, it is you who will have to show them the way. Why do you think it was you rather than I living that role in David's dream? In fact, that's part of our plan for today. I agree, Will, it is time for your family to know me and learn about their wings for themselves. I'm hoping it's that time for your friends and classmates as well. But their dreams might only happen should you awake to yours."

I nodded slowly and simply in agreement. Hearing Founder talk of my family like that was music to my ears, better than a dream if I did say so myself. I couldn't wait to bring them all here—wherever here is—and they could have their own special encounter with Founder, I'd be more than happy to lead them to him. It'd definitely be a little easier than trying to explain him. We could rebuild our own little culture—*the right way*! I thought Mom would love him the most, might bring out the lively side of her again, and Dad would get there as well, once he got past the initial shock. Founder would be just what David needed. I could hardly keep my mind from racing forward; ideas and possibilities just kept on coming, having been clogged up for most of my life the "free" button had certainly been pushed.

"Ok, slow down, Will. I'm really thrilled you want them all to meet me, and I would be honored to know them as well, to know anyone whom you care about in fact. But that's just not exactly how it works."

"I don't get it Founder, I…what do you mean?"

"Will, your family, your friends and classmates cannot come here on their own, and you can't literally bring them to me, no matter how much you or I desire them to. *You* have been given this special privilege—though the privilege has been mine as well—to come and journey with me in your dreams. But they will have to meet me inside you. They must see me in you. It's up to you to reveal me and make me come alive for them too. They will feel my wings rise up underneath them as you continue to let my wings rise up in you. You are our introduction, Will, and today is your graduation from—perhaps better yet, *towards*—your dreams. Dreams that mean much more than the nighttime adventures we have here."

I didn't know what to say.

"Nooo!" I shouted. "I won't have it!" I guess I knew what to say after all. "Founder, I can't. I can't lose you. I can't do this without you! I…"

"Will, I understand. But regardless of the challenge, I don't want to hear you say that nasty word can't even one more time, especially knowing how much more you carry inside, unseen to yourself. There is no *can't*. There is only *will*. I am not asking if you can, I know the answer to that question. I am asking if you will?"

I slouched down to the ground, my hands stretched across my face with tears beginning to fight their way out. Trying to live out this kind of life felt hard enough knowing Founder was there to return to, these dreams meant everything. I had a pretty good day with my family and all, but that was only knowing I'd get to visit Founder again soon. I wasn't ready to lose him. He was the fuel that was finally making my tank full enough to get up and go. No car runs without fuel of some kind, and now I'm supposed to go farther than I ever had, and on my own, without him available to fill me up? I just couldn't see it. As much as I wanted to, it seemed too daunting. I am just one person, *one*.

"I'll always be with you, Will. Remember, didn't you say that you would introduce your family and I? It's just that I will be a little less seen, and a little more lived by you—you get to bring me to life whenever and however you choose. You weren't in David's dream just to lead him to me, but to represent me. I am not your fuel Will, only true freedom can do that. Freedom isn't to be consumed, or worshipped; freedom should be the fuel to propel you forward. Freedom is a choice, not an achievement. This is the vision you're being awakened to, a renewed freedom that spreads like wildfire, wings that spread from within you and cause others to give up the weight of the world that they carry so that they too may truly fly. I will be as present as you decide me to be, as you allow me to live through you."

"So many have fallen into the trap that I once did. Too many are striving to climb the ladders of success to find the perch I once settled for. But, Will, why would one need to live in a culture of ladders if they already have their wings? They simply need to be reminded how to fly. Remember what I learned from my scars; freedom is not for the heights you can reach, but for the privilege of flying wherever the skies may take you. In those skies you will find the highest of heights, but may not even care when compared with the sheer enjoyment of getting to freely spread your wings. There is joy simply in *being who you have been created to be*. You're an eagle, Will. Don't aspire to less than who you already are. Live! Fly! Believe!"

I took a couple of deep breaths and looked back up at Founder as renewal now tried to fight its way back up in me, like a pond suddenly squeezing back into a rushing river. I knew what he said to be true. I had seen it now with my own eyes too many times not to let go. It was much more easily seen here than lived there. Perhaps believing is seeing though. Like a pilot gets his wings, I suppose I was getting my dreams, that is, if I could keep from letting skeptical, realist-centered, fearful eyes take over again. Most of me was pretty sure what I *wanted*, and that was to stay in my dreams, not necessarily have them just yet. Such talk of dreams—or living them—was easy when it was talk. But to actually grab hold of them and paint them into reality would mean I'd have to start stroking my brush upon this new, blank canvas my life had become—like every moment mattered. Just saying it to myself made me want it more though. It meant I had to pioneer my own path in the skies, and somehow, I'd have to show others how they too could learn to fly. But, how could I without Founder?

I was genuinely conflicted, even though I felt my spirit rising, I still had the potential to be my own worst enemy. I started to look down, mirroring where my doubts wanted to take me, but they were in a dogfight with my will. I might have been looking through doubt, but there was a renewed hope and vision peering out from behind my eyes, trapped like an innocent captive, determined to see his way through. A deep sigh pushed its way out, hands to my head. I was right back at the same question—*how?*

"Will, the Liberty Bell cracked while it was ringing.

It's the same with freedom. It developed a crack somewhere along the way while ringing loudly, but the crevice within freedom has become more like a canyon now, large enough for much of culture to easily fall into. The wolves falsify a hopeful path across, but it only leads people further down said crevice, further into darkness, further from true vision. Remember, that is why you are a bridge. You can help seal that crack in freedom by the way you choose to live. The bell might not ring anymore to the world's ear, but you can hear it in your dreams. Similarly, true freedom doesn't ring a whole lot anymore, at least not the way it used to, or through as many as it once did. Freedom too stands there as a monument we try to hold onto—cracks and all. But freedom's sound can still be revived." Founder's passion rose with cause, and I couldn't help but notice he appeared to be staring directly at the cause in me.

"If people only knew the potential of true freedom, you know what would happen, Will? It could ring loud once again, loud enough to awaken a nation out of a slumbering culture and into a renewed dream. But make no mistake about it, *it will have to ring through you.*"

"Founder, I've been journaling after every dream, taking notes so that I wouldn't forget a thing. I can go down the list, but a checklist isn't going to do squat for me now. I'm sorry to be blunt, but it's too important. I don't want to coast in the new and waste it like I did before. *How* do I let my life ring like that? How do I live freedom without the cracks? What is more, if I do, how will they even hear me?"

"Will, it is in the little things. Mostly, it is how you live towards people on a consistent basis. It's how you live out your newfound vision and perspective, and how you make your beliefs come to life even when they don't seem to come naturally to you; pushing through the fear knowing that light will soon break in. Such life is choosing to live from the Ridge of Hope every day, telling fear where you stand for the sake of seeing life from a higher perspective. You can't lose heart, nor can you ever allow anyone to take your hope. How can they if it stems from inside you? To let your freedom ring is to be that light in the darkness, and seeing others with that light, even if you're the only bulb in the room. It's not turning off or dimming yourself to blend in and never apologizing for what the darkness might call blinding, that just means the wolves are afraid that many more will use your light to once again see what the wolves have stolen."

"Will, do you remember at Dr. King's memorial, when I asked you to deliver your own 'dream' speech? Well, your life is your opportunity, within every day and every conversation—*live out loud!* It takes courage to live such a speech, far more courage than it would take you to deliver one. Dr. King did both! You don't need a memorial in your honor to build upon the legacy of someone such as Dr. King; you just need courage to keep living out loud when the world is quiet and afraid to learn a new song. Let your life burn passionately with uncompromising kindness, love that doesn't need a vocabulary, and actions that light the fire in others, even when those around you try and lie dormant with barely a crackle. Dr. King's speech lives on through you, but it will be felt in an even greater, widespread diversity of ways as more people choose to live out such a dream. *That* takes courage."

"As we've discussed, and you've well discovered on your own, it's not easy. It requires perseverance to live a river life. You have to learn to be unmoved in your heart, even when others might fear losing ground in their territory. Change can ruffle feathers so don't be harsh but walk in peace. Remember, a river carries moving, living water with nutrients that cannot be found in a pond. As they watch the life you bring they will eventually start to understand. But for this to happen you have to keep moving forward and pioneering such a path for the sake of their dreams. The river life is a tension of pressure from the outside world, but as long as you walk with Peace in the river then it doesn't matter how differently you live. Twist or turn, your life, as the river does, will bring life-giving change wherever you go. Don't submit to the pressures of the wolves, remember, they're bullies who are truly more afraid than you. They just haven't had many who have confronted them with the real, life-giving pressure of the river through their land often enough to let their true darkness be known. If enough of you live this way, you'll see the difference for yourself."

"Will, you ring loud naturally when you choose to live differently, different from the path culture attempts to convince you is the only way. It's not. Every choice before you is your opportunity to be clear about whether you yourself will be consumed by the wolves of culture, or if you will go against their grain and prove there is a different way, an unseen truth and a better life to be had. You can bring life back to your neighborhood and help remove the masks that lack laugh lines, a place where you can love people by name. It's you who gives value to such a culture; a culture that sometimes only waits for one domino to fall, someone who will stand up and demand a home-cooked meal."

"That's where you get to become such a diverse family, appreciating the differences in one another and coming together beyond likeness, and simply out of love. It's a different love than most know, a love that honors each person not for what they can do, have done, or where they come from or are going. It's the kind of honor that believes the best, doesn't keep a record of wrongs and pulls out the gold from that very place of difference in each life. Freedom lets you find the promise in one another and recognize that it's a much greater treasure than anything anyone could ever achieve. Such promise is waiting in your neighbors everywhere, waiting to be seen and given value. The majority of people will never speak out such a need for even a second, but that surely doesn't mean that they aren't waiting. Everyone wants to be loved, valued and believed in. Be that someone for them. Help them find their own unique wings and that place of difference where those wings might be buried inside."

"Will, don't be fooled by the glass box all around. It gives you the impression of freedom as you can look through it for miles, but from within it there is actually nowhere to go. The vultures of the world are patient creatures that will out wait all your toil. It's a false freedom, with false vision; a hologram of itself and the very crack we speak of. In the box you will find the counterfeit version of almost everything good that can be had. Counterfeit may appear real, but in the end, when you go to pay the price you find out that you've spent everything, time, treasure and talents on something that truly had no worth at all. There is more, but it's underneath the surface."

"And remember, money can never buy you freedom, no matter what it or anyone else says. It can be a useful tool, but when it starts to outweigh the people and purpose in our lives then we have to check our scale again. Prosperity is a gift this country has been given. True freedom will only exponentially multiply such a gift when used for the new beginnings this dream was originally built for. Providence is power packed with second chances, grace, mercy and forgiveness, but true prosperity is never found in money but in the abundance within. It's what helps you spread your wings. If you combine the providence of your great nation with the vision you're beginning to see life through, you will yourself possess a generosity of spirit that begins to buy back a culture of dreams that lead the sheep to follow the right voice. You will help to buy back their lives with the value you esteem."

"Perfection is never the goal, Will, nor do I ever expect it of you. As I shared before, even your scars—well, especially your scars—will give you far more than your greatest victories, so don't be afraid to try for the fear of falling, or failing. All I ask is that your fall doesn't come from a perch amidst competing heights, but from the sky while learning to once again spread your wings. I would never judge you for one of your scars, Will, just as you don't judge me for mine. They are what has given me the opportunity to influence your life, my scars give me the joy of helping to redeem your dreams."

"This Liberty Bell has its own scars now, as does the freedom your culture has put on a perch. From that high perch, freedom can give very little to a nation of sheep. But when it spreads its wings through those like you there is no limit to the heights it may soar and how it may exponentially grow. Over the years you have become a culture that resembles this bell with all your scars and stripes. You have hung at the noose of what you once were, trying to hold on and maintain the bronze image the wolves have claimed happiness to be. But Will, it's time for your bell to toll again and rejoin your founders' original pursuit. It's time for you to be awakened from the dream you have been taught to live, and breathe hope to a world that unknowingly waits for true freedom to ring once more. It's the freedom to actually live a renewed dream. That bell, when found in enough of those like you, will ring loud enough to awaken the nation."

I couldn't tell if Founder had finished or been interrupted, for at that moment I heard the bell ring. After all these years of silence, the crack in the bell became but a scar and freedom resumed its sound. I stood there listening in awe, watching the bell move and divine its own anthem, mesmerized by its angelic noise like none I had ever heard before.

Founder's eyes glared deeply—hopefully—into mine. But I couldn't pull myself away to look at him, for the bell had captured my attention and I couldn't take my eyes off the crack. To see the crack while listening to the sound of the bell only amplified the power that was beginning to ring through my life. *The crack made it better*, but only after it was renewed. The scar-ish crack gave it a shot at redemption, a depth of wisdom learned, and the hope to ring even louder. And I now believed I could live the very same.

****

The shaking continued, only now it was in the disarray of my very own bed. The bell was still ringing only now Founder was gone, and there was no

Philadelphia. The bell had morphed into my alarm clock, as if it had been synched with my dreams it now woke me to get out of bed and realize the choices presented before me that day. I had been awakened from one old, hopeless dream to the privilege of meeting Founder, who led me on many nighttime adventures that still, and probably always would grasp my heart.

I looked down as I rose from my bed and there on my pillow was one single feather that could only have been plucked from Founder himself. Next to it was my favorite childhood toy, still worn and chipped from the many days of play; a superhero that as a child once gave me the hope I later lost. I didn't yet know the meaning of the toy or its sudden redemption, but it certainly brought back vivid memories of my adolescence and a season of life when I was convinced that I too could transform a dim culture. I never got to say goodbye to Founder, an unceremonious ending to our relationship. But I knew he was here. I would make sure of it. He had never left my side, and now, I would never leave his. I was awakened so I could introduce him to the world, with hope that they too might learn, if not remember, how to dream, again.

"One of the great liabilities of history is that all too many people fail to remain awake through great periods of social change. Every society has its protectors of status quo and its fraternities of the indifferent who are notorious for sleeping through revolutions. Today, our very survival depends on our ability to stay awake, to adjust to new ideas, to remain vigilant and to face the challenge of change."

- Dr. Martin Luther King Jr.

ABOUT THE AUTHOR

Joey, his wife, Destiny, and their five children live just outside of Denver, CO. Joey is the author of five books, each of which empower the reader to see differently, live differently, and love differently. You can find him writing in coffee shops near and far, wherever good espresso may be found. Though Joey enjoys writing in various forms, he finds a unique reality waiting to be found through stories of parabolic and allegorical means.

www.joeyletourneau.com
joey.letourneau@gmail.com